The Sultan of Zanzire

Ben Westerham was born in 1964 in London. After many years spent writing in bits and pieces, Ben now primarily writes crime, mystery and thriller fiction, often with a healthy serving of humour. He lives in rural Northamptonshire in the English Midlands.

The
Sultan
of
Zanzire

BEN WESTERHAM

Ben Westerham asserts the moral right to be
identified as the author of this work

Published by Close9 Publishing

ISBN: 978-1-911085-87-4

ALSO BY BEN WESTERHAM

ALEXANDER TEMPLEMAN SERIES
The House of Spies
The Meyer-Hoffman Affair

BANBURY CROSS MURDER MYSTERY SERIES
The Hide and Seek Murders
The Club of Death
The Hobby Horse Murder
A Legacy of Death
The Golf Club Murder
Death of a Scarecrow

DAVID GOOD PRIVATE INVESTIGATOR SERIES
Good Investigations
The Strawberry Girl
Good Girl Gone Bad
Too Good to Die
Smart Way to Die
The Good Con
Good and the Vanishing Act
As Good as Dead

SHORTS IN THE DARK SERIES
Harry Minch
Memory of Murder
Lesson for a Thief
Collector of Crimes
Shattered Dreams

50FOR30 MICRO SHORTS SERIES
50for30 Series One
50for30 Series Two

MULTI-AUTHOR ANTHOLOGIES
Breakneck

ACKNOWLEDGMENTS

Because I don't do it often enough, I'd like to express my love and my thanks to my wife, Joanne, for, without her endless support and encouragement, none of these books would ever have seen the light of day.

And a dollop of thanks to those who have gone before me and have been my guide and inspiration.

IT'S ALL ENGLISH TO ME

A word on the language that's used in this book, so you know what to expect. The version of English that is used here is British. This ought not to present much in the way of a problem for non-British readers. If you do find the occasional word or phrase a little odd, then I hope you still understand the essence of what is being said.

***

"Pardon,' he said, 'I'm a bit rattled tonight. You see, I happen at this moment to be dead."

The Thirty-Nine Steps, John Buchan

* * *

CONTENTS

1	A New World Beckons	1
2	Trouble in Zanzire	8
3	A New Assignment	16
4	A Journey South	23
5	The Eternal City	27
6	Plans Are Altered	33
7	Meeting The Ambassador	35
8	An Agent Bearing News	41
9	A New Relationship Forms	46
10	The Fox's Lair	54
11	A Master Entertainer	56
12	A Lavish Affair	63
13	A Shocking Encounter	68
14	Darkness Descends	75
15	Welcome News	79
16	A Pursuit, At Last	85
17	A Confrontation Erupts	91
18	The Aftermath	97
19	The British Embassy	100
20	The Villa Carlotta	104
21	Desperate News	108
22	Disaster	112
23	A Prisoner	116
24	Interrogation	122
25	A Bid for Freedom	126
26	An Opportunity	131
27	An Explosive Encounter	134
28	The Patient	137
29	A Sighting is Reported	142
30	The Farm	146
31	A Plan is Hatched	149
32	The Net Closes	151
33	The Escape	155
34	A Pair of Hunting Hounds	159

35	A Welcome Confrontation	165
36	Where Death Lingers	169
37	A Final Showdown	171
38	The Horn of Africa	175

A NEW WORLD BECKONS

"Look out, Templeman."

The shouted warning came from my right, out of a cluster of densely packed pine trees. The voice seemed familiar, though I couldn't quite put a name to it, and I instinctively turned my head in search of whoever it was that had called out. That was a mistake, one I recognised a fraction of a second too late. There was a sudden movement behind me, an awareness of a rushing breeze, then a violent contact with the side of my head.

I awoke to find myself tangled in a bed sheet, sprawled across the bedroom floor. I had fallen out of bed. My right elbow ached, as did the side of my head. I cursed and began to extricate myself from the clutches of the sheet, which seemed, on its part, to be doing its best to resist such efforts.

The dream I had been having was not a new one. Indeed, it had plagued my efforts at sleep for the previous five nights, and was, I had determined, an unsettling reminder of how close I had come to losing my life on a recent assignment attempting to keep Professor Meyer-Hoffman from the clutches of the German secret service.

It was fortunate that my wife, Caroline, was staying with her parents. She had become rather alarmed at my recent habit of awaking in the night with a start, my forehead thick with sweat and my heart rate rapid. She had suggested more than once that I should consult our doctor about the matter.

As I climbed to my feet I noticed the first dull light of the approaching dawn seeping around the edges of the curtains. It was a little after six. As my aches began to ease, I laid back down on the bed and attempted to distract my mind. I began to contemplate the lecture I was due to attend that afternoon, but soon found myself wondering if Caroline might not be right after all. Perhaps a consultation with our doctor was, indeed, in order.

*

I was, to my embarrassment, a little late arriving at the lecture theatre and was obliged to make my way, as discretely as possible, to a vacant seat in the last row of chairs. I say discretely, but my cheeks were warmed a little by the unwelcome realisation that the person standing at the lectern had observed my arrival. I removed my hat and coat before sitting down and smiled apologetically at an elderly gentleman in the next seat, who looked a good deal less than pleased at the interruption.

The lecture theatre was a sizeable affair, the largest available within the Department of History at St Michael's College. It's construction had been completed two years previously, in the June of 1911, barely twelve months after the college had become part of London University. Despite its considerable size, the room was close to full, with an audience that a quick survey of the room suggested came from all walks of life; a very large number of them women. All appeared to be enraptured by the speaker, whose combination of solid authority and beguiling charm exerted a strong hold over the crowd.

Miss Catherine Bachini's lecture on the subject of ancient Athens had been most enthusiastically recommended to me by an old friend, who had heard her speak the previous year. 'Captivating' was the word he kept falling back on, when describing her performance, and I could at once see why. There was a passion for her subject matter in her voice that was hard to miss and a glow in her eyes that held you at once, along with a delivery that told a story rather than presented us with cold, hard facts. I began to think that I might, perhaps, have been content to hear her lecture on any subject, no matter how uninspiring I might ordinarily find it.

I knew from my friend that Miss Bachini was Anglo-Italian. Her father, a diplomat of some repute, had met her mother while he was assigned to the Italian embassy in London. She had, I was also told, attended Durham University, where she read history and archaeology. Apart from that, I knew precious little about her, other than that she had spent time as a young girl in first England and then the United States before her father was called back to Italy. I did, though, make a mental note to thank my friend for his fine recommendation.

The hour I spent listening with rapt attention passed in what felt like half the time, so enthralled was I. Indeed, when the lecture came to its conclusion I felt somewhat saddened.

"Quite a remarkable performance, for a woman," remarked the old fellow who had given me such a disapproving look earlier. "Even seems to know her stuff, which, I must say, I wasn't at all expecting. Young people today seem to believe all it takes to become an expert on a topic is to read a few books and nothing more. I must assume Miss Bachini's lecturers at Durham were of the finest quality."

I might have engaged the man in a little conversation, but I'd barely replied that I agreed on the calibre of the lecture when he picked up his coat and departed. As the rest of the audience swarmed all around me, the sound of their conversations rising, I glanced up at the large, round clock set high on the wall at the back of the theatre. It was a little after noon and I had an awkward hour to dispose of before meeting Whitney Willard Straight, a one-time colleague of mine, for luncheon. Whitney had inherited a rather tidy sum upon the death of his only aunt at the start of the year and had immediately taken to a life of sloth and indolence in a rather whole-hearted manner. But, to be fair to the fellow, he was most generous in sharing his new-found wealth with his friends.

I had not the time to return home and had no pressing missions to accomplish that I could assign the hour to. There was, I had noticed, a tea room at the front of the building and, with little else to do, I decided to while away the time there, reading the newspapers.

But peering in through the window, it looked rather busy and I was hesitating about entering when I heard a voice call out, "Alexander. Alexander, it is you."

Margaret Swinton was the sister of one of my old school friends, Justin Hinchwood. It had been two or perhaps even three years since I had last seen her. Hinchwood had assured me on many an occasion in the past that Margaret had rather a crush on me, something I had taken considerable care not to encourage. She was, how to put this politely, rather too strong a character for me to consider spending the rest of my days with. I'd heard via a mutual acquaintance that she had been married the previous year, to the youngest son of a knight of the realm, whose name escapes me.

"Margaret, what an unexpected pleasure," I replied, as I turned around. "Were you here for the lecture by any chance?"

"Absolutely."

"I didn't know the Ancient Greeks were an interest of yours," I remarked.

"They're not particularly, but I'd been assured the opportunity to attend one of Catherine Bachini's lectures should be grabbed with both hands, so here I am, and I'm jolly glad I came along."

"Yes, she was very good," I responded. "Charismatic, as well as highly knowledgeable."

"It was really rather pleasing to see a woman give such a well-attended and excellently-received lecture, even if I didn't fully understand parts of it. Who knows, we women might actually get the vote one of these days and then we'll see a change or two in this male-dominated world of ours," I was assured in a most forceful manner.

I managed a half-smile, feeling a little awkward. The topic of female emancipation was not one I was entirely comfortable with, even if I was broadly sympathetic to the notion. My wife, Caroline, is most insistent the day is almost upon us and not before time, as far as she is concerned, whereas I am rather more conservative in my outlook on such things and would prefer to ease more gently into such a major change.

"Of that I have no doubt whatsoever," I replied, not sure I was keen to hear what changes might be on her agenda. "Though I fear there remain one or two important people in the corridors of Parliament who are yet to be persuaded as to the desirability of feminine emancipation."

"Fear not, we'll turn them to our view of things, one way or the other," she replied with an unsettling twinkle in her eyes. "But do tell me how… Oh, here comes Miss Bachini. Oh, we really must have a moment of her time. Miss Bachini," Margaret called out as she waved a hand in a very energetic manner.

Catherine Bachini stood little chance of avoiding the summons and gave in gracefully, joining us outside the tea rooms. I would like to say that I engaged her in some thought-provoking conversation on the subject of her lecture, but the truth is that, after the usual introductions, Margaret did rather dominate matters.

This did, however, provide me with an opportunity to make a more considered appraisal of Miss Bachini. At once I had to admit to myself that I had not done her complete justice when it came to her beauty. Her mouth was somewhat small, her nose a little on the large size and her eyebrows perhaps a little thicker than I would consider ideal, but the whole, framed by dark brown hair with a pleasing natural curl, was undeniably beautiful. And now that she was standing in front of me, those brown eyes of hers, deep and filled with something I could only describe as passion, were mesmerising. It was hard not to stare.

Her tolerance and good humour in dealing with the barrage of questions from Margaret was also impressive, never once showing any sign of irritation or a desire to be elsewhere, despite the banality of some of the enquiries and observations. I've no doubt that most male academics would have recoiled in bad temper from such an imposition.

I had, in fact, assumed such a position of silent observation that when Miss Bachini turned her attentions on me, I was caught rather off guard and ill prepared to provide an answer.

"And you, Mr Templeman, are you much acquainted with the history of Ancient Greece?" she asked. "Or do your true interests lie elsewhere?"

"Ancient Greece?" I repeated, my mind racing to catch up. "I'm afraid to say I know no more than the little we were taught at school, though it is a subject I have long wished to learn more about, hence my attendance at your excellent lecture."

"Thank you and I'm glad you enjoyed it. You didn't find it too lacking in academic discipline? Too accessible for the amateur enthusiast?"

She smiled beguilingly as she spoke and there was a playfulness in her voice that suggested she was teasing me. I gathered that she had, in all likelihood, faced some criticism from the old fuddy duddies of the academic world in regard to her success in engaging an inexpert audience on her specialist subject.

"Not at all," I replied, fashioning something of a smile myself. "In my opinion, for what it's worth, I thought you achieved a most agreeable balance, conveying some serious observations in a manner even someone like me could understand."

She laughed, in a most disarming manner, which left Margaret looking somewhat confused. "I should wheel you in front of some of my older and more conservative colleagues," Bachini said, "They seem to think that the public at large are not capable of taking on board an understanding of any history much beyond what they ate for breakfast this morning."

I would have liked to have continued the conversation, but Margaret decided I had exhausted my allocation of time and took back a firm grip on proceedings with a question about the facilities available for women studying at university. A short while after this, Miss Bachini wished us both a pleasant day and departed, though her presence lingered a while longer. As for me, I pleaded the need to be on my way to my luncheon with Whitney, whom I was due to meet at his club, Greens, and thereby escaped the clutches of Margaret Swinton.

I mention this encounter with the beautiful and talented Catherine Bachini because, though I didn't know it at the time, it was to prove a precursor to events of a far more serious nature in the weeks ahead. I suppose that, had we both known of its significance at the time, our conversation would have been of a very different nature. But I ought not to get too far ahead of myself, or I will risk causing you, the reader, a good deal of confusion.

As it was, I departed for my luncheon with Whitney Willard Straight pleased to have attended Miss Bachini's lecture and delighted to have met her, if but briefly, afterwards. She was, perhaps, a living, breathing example of the future that Margaret Swinton had so enthusiastically alluded to and I wondered if the world was, in fact, prepared for such changes.

TROUBLE IN ZANZIRE

Eight days had passed since I attended Miss Bachini's fine lecture and I was now waiting outside the office of Sir Joshua Childers, head of the Secret Intelligence Bureau and, thereby, my superior. I had been warned that he was not in the best of moods, having been forced to spend much of the morning with the Home Secretary after being accosted during one of his not infrequent and lengthy visits to our nondescript office. Thus I sat in a restless, nervous silence opposite his busy secretary.

When the door to Sir Joshua's office swiftly swept open, it left me not a little startled as it was the normal practice of the head of the Bureau to summon his visitors via a button wired through to a buzzer on his secretary's desk.

"Ah, there you are Templeman," declared Sir Joshua, in his usual deep, clear voice, as he stood in the doorway. "Well, don't loiter out there, man. Get yourself in here. Eastwood should be along shortly."

Vivian Eastwood was our chief of intelligence gathering and he more often than not attended briefings with Sir Joshua, since he was central to the operations of the Bureau. His presence pointed towards our meeting being one of significance and I began to anticipate a new assignment.

As the door closed behind us, Sir Joshua took his seat behind his large, oak desk and I one of the high-backed chairs in the middle of the room. Sir Joshua was a short, plump man with a chubby face dominated by a somewhat old-fashioned bushy moustache that he twiddled as he sat back in his chair.

"How's that wife of yours, Caroline, getting along?" he asked, rather brightly. "Not been put off by your more undesirable domestic habits, I hope. I imagine you've had to start making a few changes since getting married. No more arriving home in the small hours or loitering in bed beyond a reasonable hour of a morning."

He sounded rather amused, far from the grumpy individual I had been expecting, and I felt myself relax a good deal.

"Caroline is a most understanding woman," I replied. "I do believe she has had to make rather more accommodations and changes to her normal habits and routines than have I. However, it's true, I have been leaving social engagements somewhat earlier than I once would have done."

"Well, I've no doubt she will have you all ship shape and operating to a proper routine soon enough. I know it didn't take Lady Childers long to sort me out," he added, with some amusement.

There was a solid rap on the door and Sir Joshua called out for the new arrival to enter.

"Good afternoon, Sir Joshua," announced Vivian Eastwood as he strode into the room. "Templeman. Glad to see you're on time."

Sir Joshua gestured for Eastwood to take a seat before leading us straight into business. "Now then, I'm sure you've already worked out that I've not called you here today for a social visit, Templeman. Far from it. There are vitally important developments taking place that, if not managed correctly, could have some pretty dire consequences for the country and the Empire. Word has reached us of a most serious threat that we must address as a matter of some urgency."

Sir Joshua looked directly at Eastwood and gave a little nod of the head. The chief of intelligence gathering got to his feet and unrolled a map that he had brought along with him, pinning it to a section of the wooden panelling on the wall.

"As you can see, Templeman, this is a map of the Middle East and North-Eastern Africa and right here," Eastwood added, tapping a cane on a spot towards the middle of the sheet, "you will observe, is the Suez Canal, which is, it doesn't need me to remind you, a vitally important communications channel for us."

It was a little awkward getting a clear sight of the map from where I was sitting, so I got to my feet and joined Eastwood, peering attentively at the part of the world he was pointing to.

"Of course," I replied. "Our route to India and all that lies beyond."

"Quite so. Now, look here," commanded Eastwood, as if he was still addressing a room full of subordinates in an Army briefing. "See these areas coloured in dark blue?"

"Two at the mouth of the Red Sea and that larger area on the Horn?" I replied.

"That's right and there are a few much smaller areas of territory along the southern coast of Arabia, most of the rest of which we have control over," added Eastwood, tapping his cane several times in the vicinity of Aden. "They are the territories, the few that remain, of the Sultan of Zanzire."

I looked quizzically at Eastwood. "The Sultan of Zanzire, you say. I don't believe I am familiar with that sultanate. He's not subject to the Ottomans, I take it?" I asked, hesitantly.

"Indeed he is not. The sultanate was established in 1719 and grew rapidly for a time, its territories extending further down the Horn than they do now and reaching some way inland to what is now Italian Somalia. The territory has been steadily whittled away since the early part of the last century, the current Sultan's grandfather losing the Somalia lands in a disastrous attempt to extend further inland in the 1830s. The last Sultan did his best to steady the ship, but he wasn't a particularly impressive man and the sultanate continued to shrink. If not for the talents of the current Sultan, it would probably have disappeared altogether by now."

"But the Sultan seems to have kept control of some rather important parcels of land," I remarked, gesturing towards the map.

"He has indeed," replied Eastwood. "Erteria, in particular, offers a controlling position over the entrance to the Red Sea," he said, resting the tip of his cane against the relevant portion of the map. "And the island of Adotra, off the coast of Aden, does almost as good a job, even though it is a little further away."

"What about the larger part of his territory, on the Horn?"

Eastwood pulled his cane away from the map and began tapping it in his other hand. "Yemeenia, on the eastern coast of the Horn, is where his capital, Addis Mara, is located. Despite its size, it's a rather poor part of the world, not as well placed for trade as the other territories."

"And the bits and pieces along the southern Arabian coast?" I enquired, keen to complete the tour.

"Little more than fishing villages, every last one of them. Used to be a solid strip of land at one time, but the sultanate gradually lost its grip," Eastwood replied.

"I suppose, under the circumstances, the Sultan has done rather well to keep a grasp on any of his remaining lands," I suggested, peering in closer so as to better make out the tiny dark blue dots that had been marked on the southern Arabian coast.

"That's true enough. However, it's a situation that it appears is about to change." Eastwood took a step back from the map before continuing. "In an effort to modernise his territories, especially their administrative apparatus and the armed forces, such as they are, the Sultan accepted a loan from the Kaiser's government."

I raised an eyebrow in acknowledgement of this news.

Eastwood continued, "That was four years ago and the capital repayments are due to begin next year. Since the Sultan has already been experiencing difficulties in making the interest payments, all concerned fully expect that he will not be able to meet the additional commitments and thereby default on the loan."

I looked again at the map, my mind starting to work through the implications of such an outcome.

"As you may already have surmised," said Eastwood. "The loan is, in effect, a mortgage over the Sultan's territories."

"And the Germans would be delighted to seize Erteria and, perhaps, also Adotra," I suggested.

"Quite. The former in particular would provide them with an excellent strategically important position from which they would be able to disrupt our shipping movements up and down the Red Sea, should the anticipated war break out," pointed out Eastwood, little lines appearing on his forehead.

"We, of course," piped up Sir Joshua, "are most keen they don't get their grasping little hands on the Sultan's territories. Would be something close to a disaster if they were to succeed in that."

"Are we not able to intercede?" I asked, addressing the head of the bureau. "Surely we could provide the Sultan with a new loan?"

"That would be the simplest of solutions, Templeman, you're absolutely right about that. Trouble is, the matter has already become a rather complicated affair and one not without its risks. The French and Italians, you see, are both laying claim to Erteria. The French already having territory to the south in French Somalia and the Italians to the north in Italian Eritrea. The Germans, for their part, have been threatening to send in gun boats if either of them makes a move to occupy Erteria."

"And that could precipitate a wider war in the region and possibly here in Europe," I observed.

"Indeed it could," replied Sir Joshua. "And one also has to acknowledge the role of the Sultan. He is, it is clear, feeling hemmed in and in need of a friend, but he's no fool and understands the strength of his current position, despite the need to repay the German loan."

Sir Joshua looked to Eastwood to pick up the story once more.

"Both the French and Italians have discreetly offered to provide the Sultan with a new loan," he began. "One on better terms than they currently enjoy. This would, of course, allow them to pay off the Germans. But the Sultan has yet to accept either offer as he feels, it seems, he may be able to extract better terms from the forthcoming negotiations."

"Negotiations?" I asked.

"His Majesty's Government is keen to avoid this dispute turning into a war," replied the head of intelligence gathering. "And to stop the Germans from taking the territories at the Red Sea entrance. The Foreign Secretary has offered to facilitate a conference to bring the matter to a mutually agreeable settlement. Whilst the Germans have shown themselves reluctant to attend, the Sultan has left them little choice, making it clear he has offers of alternative loans at his disposal. Indeed, he rather snapped up the offer of a conference, no doubt confident he will leave it on terms highly favourable to himself."

"You understand, Templeman," cut in Sir Joshua. "That our sole aim in all this is to keep the territories at the mouth of the Red Sea out of the hands of the Germans. Anything else is a minor matter of relatively little interest to us."

"Quite so, Sir Joshua."

"The Italians have offered to host the conference," said Eastwood. "An offer the Sultan has insisted all parties accept. A venue in the hills just outside Rome has been agreed, as have the dates for the conference, which will take place between the 16th and 18th of October; so not long to go."

I rubbed a hand over my chin as I took on board what I had been told. "And do I take it you want me to play some minor part at this conference?" I asked, not at all certain what role I could possibly be at all well-equipped to play.

Sir Joshua's face darkened. "I'm afraid to say word has reached us that an attempt may be made on the life of the head of the Italian delegation, the Count of Villafranca. Should that happen, it would be certain to bring the negotiations to a swift and chaotic end, and leave the Germans in a position of unassailable strength, able to call in their loan the moment the Sultan defaults."

"These threats are credible?" I asked.

"As far as we can determine," replied Sir Joshua. "At the same time, the Germans have been talking up the right of the Sultan to determine his own future and the respect he deserves as a great leader in the region. This will all be in an effort to ingratiate themselves, of course. There has also been a steady stream of malicious rumours doing the rounds seeking to drive a bigger wedge between the French and Italians, which we strongly suspect are being promulgated by the Germans."

"So, they are doing what they can to either put an end to the conference before an agreement can be reached or else to undermine our attempts to shepherd the Italians and French into an agreed resolution," I summarised.

"Absolutely," confirmed Sir Joshua. "And that's where you come in. Vivian will provide you with a more detailed briefing after we're finished here, but, in summary, you and Stoneman will be travelling out to Italy tasked with helping the Italians to ensure there are no attempts made on the life of Count Villafranca. Ideally, you will identify any assassin so the Italians can pick him up before he can make an attempt on the Count's life. You'll have to work with an Italian agent, I'm afraid. The Italians wouldn't accept any other arrangement. Vivian will tell you more about that in his briefing."

"Sounds like quite the challenge," I observed, my mind beginning to fill with questions.

"It can't be overstated how important a successful

outcome is to this conference, Templeman. If things don't go our way then the Germans will gain a strategically important position at the mouth of the Red Sea, from where they will be able to interrupt the movement of our naval and merchant ships passing to and from India in the event of a war. We don't really mind if it's the French or the Italians who end up coming out on top, just so long as it's not the Germans. If you fail at your assignment the consequences could be disastrous."

Sir Joshua rapped his fingers on his desk, then sat back down, looking a little apprehensive.

"That's quite understood, Sir Joshua. I'm sure that, with the help of this Italian agent, Stoneman and I will be able to snuff out this threat."

"Quite so," replied the head of the Bureau, picking up his ever-present pipe and beginning to fiddle with it. "I've every faith in the pair of you. That's why you've been selected for the assignment. Now then, Vivian will provide you with more details. Best of luck, Templeman, and remember to watch your own back too."

"Thank you, Sir Joshua."

As Eastwood and I left Sir Joshua's office, I began to think of breaking the news of my imminent departure to Caroline. We were due to visit friends of hers in Somerset at the weekend, a trip she had been very much looking forward to. It seemed it would now need to be rearranged.

A NEW ASSIGNMENT

Eastwood marched me down the corridor with his customary gusto, a hangover, or so I took it, of his military days. His skills in intelligence gathering had first been spotted by Sir Joshua when they fought alongside each other in the Boer War and the chief of intelligence-gathering had been persuaded to join the Bureau upon its launch. It was difficult now to imagine the Bureau operating without him, so central had he become to its work, and Sir Joshua leaned on him a good deal.

Eastwood's office was a rather more Spartan affair than was Sir Joshua's. In fact, it was bereft of almost any ornamentation, a solitary photograph of his wife and two sons occupying a little space on his desk and a painting of Lord Roberts on the wall. Nothing was out of place. Every surface was spotlessly clean. Indeed, it was entirely possible to believe that no one ever so much as disturbed the air itself in the room.

We occupied seats either side of a modest-sized oak desk and Eastwood wasted no time in taking a slim buff folder from a drawer and passing it to me.

"Some background information on the major parties who will be in attendance at the conference," said Eastwood, in the somewhat high-pitched voice that I still found a little odd for such a tall and well-built man. "It will help you to have a read through that lot before you depart, which will be on the Tuesday morning, two days before the conference begins. You'll take the boat train from Victoria station and should get to Rome in time for a late dinner, so long as there are no serious delays along the way. There'll be a ball on the evening before the conference begins, which should give you an opportunity to meet most of the people described in the notes."

"I'll read through it as soon as we're done here," I replied, flicking through a few of the pages in the folder.

Eastwood checked the time on his gold pocket watch, a rather fine gift from his great hero, Lord Roberts. "Stoneman should be here in two minutes. He's already been given much the same introductory briefing as you, but had to attend a meeting with Scotland Yard before he could join us. Once he's here, I will provide you both with more details of the operation and answer your questions, as best I can."

"Have you ever met the Sultan of Zanzire?" I asked, "I'm curious to know what sort of a man he is."

Eastwood scratched the side of his large, hawk-like nose. "I've not had the pleasure myself, no. But Sir Joshua and I spoke to Sir Anthony Gibbins at the Foreign Office yesterday, to get a first-hand impression of the Sultan. Sir Anthony has met him on two occasions. He is, by all accounts, an intelligent and shrewd individual who has, so far, managed to navigate his way successfully through the complex and shifting web of allegiances and threats that exist in that part of the world. He was personally involved in the negotiations with the Germans for the loan that is causing him so much trouble now, which might suggest he has his limitations, but he quickly and ruthlessly put down an uprising in the south of Yemeenia the year before last, so clearly has the backbone required to rule over the sultanate."

"How has he gone about ruling over his territories?" I asked, keen to learn more.

"He succeeded his father in 1904 and has been fortunate in that his father, the fifth Sultan, who wasn't in general a very impressive individual, did, nonetheless, take some steps to modernise his territories. That meant he left his son a sultanate that was in a little better shape than would otherwise have been the case. The current Sultan has looked to build on his father's work, modernising the infrastructure in his territories, particularly in the capital, Addis Mara, and expanding the clove and coconut plantations which are the basis for much of their trade."

There was a sharp rap at the door.

"Enter," barked Eastwood.

George Stoneman was a rather short, thick-set individual with light-brown hair that was already thinning on top, despite his being only thirty-one years old. We'd met several times since I'd joined the Bureau and he had come across as a somewhat serious fellow, intelligent and sharp-witted, though perhaps a little lacking in humour. My attempts, on first meeting him, to find out a little about his background had been soundly rebuffed, which I had taken to indicate he wished to keep his relationships at the Bureau strictly professional.

He had several more years of experience as an agent than me, including an assignment to Constantinople that went so horribly wrong that he very nearly didn't make it back. I was told that he was left in desperate straits by a double-agent who attempted to enrich himself by informing the Ottomans of Stoneman's real reason for being in the country, which was to gather intelligence from one of our operatives. It was only by the skin of his teeth, after making full use of those sharp wits of his, that Stoneman managed to get out of the country before he was arrested, although that was not before he had been shot in the shoulder while fleeing.

Stoneman took the remaining seat in front of Eastwood's desk and, with the usual pleasantries out of the way, the head of intelligence gathering turned to the matter at hand.

"You both now have an understanding of the situation

and the importance of the forthcoming conference and you have the briefing notes I put together to provide you with more detailed information, so I shan't go over all that again. Your task is simple," continued Eastwood, his tone and demeanour most serious. "You are to identify the threat to Count Villafranca and neutralise it, preferably by handing the assassin or assassins over to the Italians. I can't overstate the importance of this matter. Should Villafranca be assassinated, it would certainly bring the conference to an end and with it would go any chance of a peaceful resolution to the situation. We know the Italians and the French have troops positioned ready to move into Erteria should there not be a satisfactory outcome and the Germans have made it clear they won't sit idly by should that happen. Their position is greatly strengthened by that blessed loan they made to the Sultan."

"Do we have any idea who is behind this threat to Count Villafranca?" asked Stoneman.

"Nothing certain, though it seems safe to assume the Germans have a hand in it somewhere, even if only indirectly. My money would be on their having arranged for a friendly party to undertake the deed for them in return for some reward. That way they could reasonably expect to be able to maintain their distance and any likelihood of being made to accept responsibility, even if we and the others do have strong suspicions."

"So, the assassins could come from anywhere," observed Stoneman, in a matter-of-fact manner.

"Indeed," responded Eastwood. "Which is why you and Templeman will need to keep your wits about you even more than usual. Now then, on to more operational matters. You will be travelling as officials of our party, there to provide administrative assistance to the British delegation. We fully expect the Germans and French will have their own agents in situ, so take care, as we expect this could turn into a rough show. You will be staying at the Garden Hotel, rather than the Embassy. The conference will be taking place at the Villa Carlotta, situated in the hills outside Rome. A rather splendid affair, by all accounts."

"We're to work with an Italian agent," I said, shifting a little towards the edge of my chair. "Do we know who this is to be?"

"I've not been given a name, if that's what you're after, but we've agreed with the Italians that their agent will meet you there and identify themselves with the code words New Spartan. He will, naturally, be your conduit to the Italian authorities and the one who will arrange for the assassin to be picked up once you've identified him, or them."

"A shame we can't know a little about this Italian agent before we meet him," I observed, not altogether happy with the arrangements.

"I agree," stated Stoneman. "It would have been preferable to have vetted their agent ahead of time. Leaves me somewhat concerned as to the quality of the individual we are asked to work with."

"It's not the arrangement I would have preferred myself," replied Eastwood. "But it's the one the Italians were insistent upon, concerned about keeping their agent under wraps for as long as possible. Since the conference is to take place on their patch, we had little choice other than to agree."

"That's understood," responded Stoneman, though there was a definite hint of unhappiness in his voice.

"Now then, as if matters weren't tricky enough, things have been somewhat complicated by the recent death of Faisal bin Turki, the Sultan of Muscat and Oman. Word reached us the day before yesterday that he died on the 4th of this month. A new Sultan," Eastwood consulted a note on his desk, "Taimur bin Feisal, has been appointed, but there has been some unrest, which the Ottomans have been busy putting down in their customary violent manner. If things should grow into something more serious it may very well have a bearing on the negotiations at the forthcoming conference, and we could do without that."

"That's unfortunate timing," observed Stoneman. "We'll be kept abreast of developments, I assume?"

"If things look like deteriorating, we'll make sure the two of you – as well as the rest of the delegation – are aware of what's happening."

There was a moment's silence in the room and into this space a thought thrust itself; one I felt I ought to have considered before.

"Do we know what the Germans consider to be the least they will settle for from the conference, irrespective of the Sultan's own position?"

Eastwood fixed his gaze on me. "It seems they are entirely confident they will get what they are aiming for and that is effective control of Erteria, whether that means a full occupation or some sort of protectorate status probably doesn't matter. I would say that, at a push, they might settle for control of the island of Adotra, but that's only my own assessment of things. We have nothing definite to go on."

"Let's hope the Sultan has sense enough to come to an arrangement with the Italians and French. That way the Germans will be in no position to demand anything," asserted Stoneman, sounding altogether more animated than he had hitherto.

"Well, if you've no other questions," began Eastwood, getting to his feet. "I've another meeting to attend shortly. Trouble also appears to be brewing in Albania and the Bureau has been asked to see if it can't get a man on the ground there. As if we're not a little stretched as it is," he added rather gruffly.

I took a step towards the door then stopped and turned back towards the head of intelligence gathering.

"There is one other thing, if you don't mind. Sir Joshua seemed a little… unsettled," I commented. "Does he fear greatly that this situation in the Red Sea might get out of hand and lead to something more dramatic?"

Eastwood fiddled with the ends of his moustache, apparently weighing his reply with some care. "It does concern him, it would be fair to say, but there are other events that are weighing on him more. The Austrian

Government passed a bill on the 3rd increasing the size of its army to 600,000 men, with authorisation for that to grow to two million if war should break out. It's difficult not to view that as a precursor to war with Serbia and thereby Russia."

"And from there the whole deck of cards falls, taking us with it," I replied, rather sombrely. "Does Sir Joshua still believe we can avert a Europe-wide war?" I asked.

Eastwood took a deep breath before replying, as if steeling himself. "It seems unlikely now, but Sir Joshua hasn't given up all hope that a peaceful outcome can be achieved. He had been rather hoping the Austrians could be persuaded not to intervene directly with Serbia, but this bill they've passed really makes that look unlikely now and I think Sir Joshua has begun to see things that way too."

"In that case, Heaven help us," commented Stoneman, as he reached for the door handle.

A JOURNEY SOUTH

Stoneman, I soon discovered, was not altogether the ideal travelling companion. My initial attempts at engaging him in a little light conversation on the train journey through Kent were rebuffed, all be it politely. Instead, I spent that leg of the journey conversing with two fascinating Belgian doctors who were returning home after spending a week in London learning about the latest developments in the treatment of cancers. I was sorry to part ways with them at Boulogne.

I saw little of Stoneman during the Channel crossing, he preferring to spend his time above decks, as he found being below decks made his stomach feel rather queasy, whereas I much preferred to relax with the newspapers inside, away from the sea spray and the heavily gusting winds.

As for the train journey across France, Stoneman spent most of it asleep in our compartment. His loud snoring hastened me along to the dining car. There, for a good while, I enjoyed the pleasant and engaging company of a young French lady and her mother, who were travelling to Italy to visit relatives in Tuscany. A most beautiful part of the world, they assured me.

However, Stoneman became a rather different chap altogether as we approached the Alps, rousing himself from his slumbers and hunting me down in the dining car, where he ordered himself a rather large meal. He was also keen to revisit, if only briefly and in the most hushed of tones, the plans we had previously agreed for our assignment.

"I must say, Templeman," he said, pushing his now empty plate to one side. "I am rather looking forward to this assignment. After the unpleasantness I experienced in Constantinople, I have been itching to get back in the field and put all that behind me. The whole messy business has been weighing on my shoulders most disagreeably ever since I got back to London."

"I can imagine," I replied. "I had a close call in Vienna myself not too long ago. My first overseas assignment. A bit of a shock to the system, I don't mind admitting. But you have considerably more experience of these matters than I do, so tell me, how do you envisage things playing out in Rome?"

"We have quite the challenge ahead of us," he said, sounding uncharacteristically animated, as he reached for his brandy. "And one where a successful outcome stands to have a real impact on world events. It's precisely the sort of thing that persuaded me to join the Bureau when Eastwood approached me. I believe the quality of the agent the Italians have assigned to work with us will be vital. So long as they have the requisite local knowledge and a capable skill set then I see no reason why we can't track down this assassin in pretty short order and put a stop to his plans."

"It's reassuring to hear you are so confident, but I do wonder if we ought not to have travelled sooner," I replied, sounding, I feared, rather grave. "We won't have a great deal of time to find this chap."

"That's true enough. But even if we'd travelled to Rome last week, it wouldn't necessarily have done us any good because there's no real reason why the assassin would need to make his own way there more than a day or two ahead of time."

The train screeched past a series of tall buildings lined up close to the track. I waited for us to clear them and for the noise to abate before picking up the conversation again.

"That's a good point and I imagine the Italians will be paying close attention to anyone who goes even remotely close to the villa where the conference is to be held. Perhaps we may pick up a pointer there," I added, hopefully.

A huge rotund man smoking a cigar began to squeeze his way along the dining carriage and, as he reached us, he paused and wished us a pleasant evening. His accent was unmistakably Germanic, though I could not say whether that was because he was German, Austrian or possibly even Swiss.

"Perhaps we ought to save further conversation on the matter for our hotel," suggested Stoneman, his gaze following the back of the cigar smoking fellow.

"A sound idea," I agreed, swirling around the brandy in my glass before downing the last of it. "Another?" I asked my fellow agent.

He nodded and I called over the waiter to order two more drinks.

"How did you square things off with your wife when you decided to sign up for this job?" I asked as I searched for something else for us to discuss.

"I'm not married," replied Stoneman, looking for a moment out of the window. "I was engaged for a time, but Emma succumbed to tuberculosis. It seemed to arrive as if from nowhere," he added, his countenance all at once darkened and I regretted my enquiry. "I've not yet been able to bring myself to look for another prospective wife and sometimes I wonder if I ever will. Perhaps it's for the best, anyway. After all, we never can be certain of making it back home from one of these assignments we are sent on."

"A valid point," I replied, feeling somewhat perplexed.

"How about you, fallen for some little woman's irresistible charms or managed to hold out so far?"

I fiddled a little with the cuff of my shirt before replying, "Recently married. I must admit, it did give me reason to hesitate before accepting the Bureau's unexpected offer, but there was a part of me that felt obliged to do my bit for King and country, especially in these dangerous times we live in."

"Well, I'm sure we'll make it safely back to London, on this occasion," Stoneman said with a little too much conviction before glancing out of the window.

For once on the journey it was I who now fell into silent contemplation and became a poor travel companion. Stoneman's observation of the risks we ran struck home, reminding me of the wonderful wife I had left behind in London and our plans for raising a fine family. He was right, of course, there was no certainty that we would make it safely back home from our assignments and, for a moment or two, I began to consider once more the merits of a life spent working in a safe if rather boring office down some nondescript side street in London.

THE ETERNAL CITY

It was dark and a little chilly by the time our train pulled into Rome's Termini railway station, both Stoneman and I a little relieved to have completed our journey. Although the concourse outside the station was still somewhat busy we had little difficulty securing a carriage to take us to the Garden Hotel and I took the opportunity to observe some of the unfamiliar sights, as best I could at such a time. I soon concluded that the morning would present a most enthralling and enticing prospect, though I feared there would be precious little time for sightseeing.

The Garden Hotel occupied a large, somewhat plain building of a more or less triangular shape on the Via Ludovisi. Its six floors looked out over a public garden on one side and what appeared to be a private villa on the other, at a junction of two roads. Along one of these ran a tram line. The hotel itself looked to be comfortable, without being ostentatious, and well-located, while also away from the busiest of areas of the city.

I thought we might perhaps find a message waiting for us, either from the Bureau or, more likely, the Embassy, but that was not the case and Stoneman and I made our way to our respective rooms to unpack what little luggage we had taken with us and to relax a little before reconvening in the hotel's bar.

The view from my window was not the spectacular sight I had hoped for, not helped by being on the second floor and, therefore, I was unable to see over the roofs of the surrounding buildings. Setting this minor disappointment to one side, I lounged on my bed for a quarter of an hour or so, then splashed a little water on my face and changed into fresh clothes before making my way downstairs to the bar.

The hotel's solitary bar was modest in size and somewhat plain in appearance, its tall, narrow windows offering a view of the street along which the tram line ran. There were no more than half a dozen other guests there who, between them, generated a soft undulating murmur of conversation. Stoneman was waiting for me, seated as far away from the other guests as possible, at a little table in the far corner, overlooked by an enormous portrait of some Italian grandee.

"I took the liberty of ordering a brandy for you," my fellow agent informed me as I pulled out a chair to sit down.

"Thank you. A quiet place," I observed, glancing over my shoulder.

"I imagine that was one of the reasons the Bureau chose the hotel," replied Stoneman. "Nothing too ostentatious that might risk attracting attention. Nor somewhere that might leave a rather sizeable hole in the Bureau's budget," he added before smiling.

"Have you been to Rome before?" I asked.

"Once, four years ago. It wasn't on Bureau business, as it happens," Stoneman answered. "My cousin, Randolph, had been undertaking a modern-day version of the Grand Tour and had been here for several days when he fell rather seriously ill. I was asked by my Uncle William to travel out and accompany Randolph back home. Except, by the time I arrived, Randolph had made a complete recovery and insisted I stay for a week before he saw me off at the Termini. I had a very pleasant time, I must say."

A little burst of laughter erupted from a group of people

sitting round a table near the entrance to the bar. An elderly woman with a mountain of grey hair and enough jewellery to open a shop appeared to be the centre of attention and enjoying it immensely.

"So, we make a start tomorrow," I said, reaching for my brandy. "Things are beginning to seem very real."

"They are indeed. As agreed, we'll call in at the Embassy first thing, so they know we've arrived safe and sound. It really would be a help if the Italian agent contacts us early tomorrow, so we can immediately set about putting in place a better plan than the one we've concocted. I fear we will be somewhat fishing in the dark until then."

"I suppose we will need to make ourselves somewhat visible if the Italian agent is going to have an opportunity to approach us discreetly," I suggested, not sure how best to do so.

"I've thought about that," replied Stoneman. "I think we ought to take coffee outside of one of the many cafes to be found hereabouts, once we've finished at the Embassy. That ought to make it easy for the Italian agent to see and approach us. I would like to think they are already aware of our arrival, so that ought not to place much of a demand on them."

"Sounds like a perfectly reasonable idea to me. I'd also like to pay a visit to the Villa Carlotta. I think it would be good for us to get the lie of the land there, as it has to be a spot the assassin will consider for his attempt on Count Villafranca's life."

"I agree. The map Eastwood put in our briefing pack shows a large tract of woodland all along the western boundary of the estate. It would appear to make an excellent approach to the villa. We ought to take a look at that and see what our Italian friends are doing to seal it off. And then there's the Count's town house. Surrounded by so many other buildings it must surely have excellent potential for an assassin."

"Very true," I agreed, though my thoughts had,

unexpectedly, insisted on drifting on to other matters.

"Something else on your mind?" asked Stoneman, clearly having read my expression.

I pursed my lips, reluctant to let the matter interfere in our discussion, but there was no point in choosing not to share my thoughts. "An old adversary," I replied. "Kurt von Luck."

"Ah, him," said Stoneman, the skin on his forehead tightening a little. "Not met the chap myself but heard a lot about him, of course. You had an unpleasant encounter with him, I understand?"

"Indeed. And I came up against his men on another assignment. When we were told to expect to see him here, in Rome, I must admit it caused my blood to rise more than a little."

"A ruthless individual, I understand," observed Stoneman, his gaze fixed sharply on me.

"Utterly," I answered, my mind reaching back to a particularly unpleasant and bloody scene on a narrow, little travelled street down by the Thames in London. "I know for certain that he killed a man in London. A cold-blooded assault motivated by nothing more than his own self-interest. I've waited some time for an opportunity to make him pay for what he did," I added, with a hint of anger in my voice, before reaching again for my drink.

Stoneman remained silent, perhaps waiting for me to let go of the frustration that had welled up so suddenly. As we sat there with our own thoughts, a party of a dozen or more entered the room. They were in fine spirits, engaged in several simultaneous, light-hearted and rather noisy conversations, and, when they made their way to a little clutch of tables adjacent to our own, it was clear that Stoneman and I would have to put an end to our talk about assassins and German agents.

Having already spent so much time in each other's company over the course of the previous day and a half, it was perhaps no surprise that we struggled to find something else to talk about. A little while later we finished our drinks and retired to our rooms, intent on getting a full night's sleep in readiness for what we expected would be a most demanding day.

*

I cast an eye over my room and saw no obvious sign of anyone having carried out a search before dropping my jacket on the bed and walking across to one of the windows. I pulled back the heavy curtain and stared out into the darkness. Here and there the cobbled street was softly lit by light that escaped through the windows of nearby buildings and I watched and listened as a solitary horse-drawn carriage made its way down the street.

Opposite the hotel, in what I took to be public gardens, all was cloaked in shadows of varying hues, save for where two street lights illuminated the ground. Standing in one of these pools of bright light I saw the figure of a man. He wore a peaked hat that hid most of his face and was smoking a pipe, swirling clouds of smoke drifting up through the light at regular intervals. At first he appeared to be expecting the arrival of another, casting a glance up and down the street, but then, as I continued to observe him, it seemed that he was in fact watching the entrance to the hotel. A tingle of unease ran up my spine.

This would not be the first time I had been placed under surveillance whilst on Bureau business but the suspicion that the arrival of Stoneman and I might already be known by our adversaries was a distinctly unsettling one. Had the German secret service got a man on constant duty at the Termini? Stoneman and I were hardly unfamiliar faces to our opposite numbers in Berlin, but would they really go to such lengths? If they had and we were now to expect to be followed everywhere we chose to go then it was going to cause us some significant inconvenience.

I shifted a little to one side, so that I was partially hidden by the curtain. It was a pointless move since the light in my room would have made me easy enough to spot the moment I had stopped by the window, but it was an instinct I could not inhibit.

As I continued to watch this shadowy figure, he looked several times more in the direction of the hotel entrance. Just as my convictions as to his motives began to settle, he became animated at the sight of a woman who must have stepped out of a side entrance and began to walk across the road towards him. They embraced, as a man and wife would, before setting off up the road and into the night.

It seemed that my imagination, perhaps enlivened by the new situation and the beginnings of a fresh adventure, had got the better of me. I felt, for a moment, a little foolish. But, as I was about to step away from the window, my eye caught a movement in the deep shadows under a large spreading tree almost directly opposite me. I lingered awhile, staring intently into the darkness. But, if there was someone out there, they gave away no further sign of their presence and I eventually pulled the curtains closed.

I tried to brush off the incident as nothing more than a case of an overly active imagination, but, as I settled into my bed a little while later, I found sleep hard to come. My mind insisted on holding on to the prospect that we might be under observation. The matter, I eventually concluded, would need to be discussed with Stoneman. It was possible we were going to need to make alterations to our plans.

PLANS ARE ALTERED

I met Stoneman in the dining room at eight o'clock sharp and, over a fine breakfast of kippers, kidneys and exceptionally strong coffee, we reviewed our schedule for the day. My fellow agent was neither overly surprised nor especially concerned by the notion that we might already be under observation. He had been expecting that to be the case. We may, he thought, need to take steps to throw any enemy agent off the scent at times we really didn't want them following us, but we would cross that bridge when we came to it.

However, Stoneman had a matter of his own to raise. He wanted my agreement to an alteration to our original plan. Eastwood's briefing notes had included details of several individuals who might prove useful to us in our hunt for the assassin. One of these was a questionable character who operated amongst the city's criminal fraternity. He was, by all accounts, well connected and a potential source of information that might help us find our quarry, though he was also not to be entirely trusted. He had English grandparents, whom he was reported to love most dearly, and was something of an Anglophile, hence his willingness to do business with the Bureau.

As he lay in bed unable to get to sleep, Stoneman had come to the not unreasonable conclusion that it would be better if one of us went in search of this character, while the other pressed ahead with the agreed visit to the British embassy. Time, he reminded me, was of the essence. I could think of no objection to this suggestion and we agreed that he would be the one to seek out the Italian, while I would meet our Ambassador. We were then to reunite at the Cafe Cosmopolitan at ten o'clock, where we would compare notes.

As for myself, I was still feeling unsettled by the notion that we might be under observation and so suggested to Stoneman that we leave the hotel several minutes apart and take the trouble to set off in different directions. He smiled a little at the idea, but agreed it was not an unreasonable precaution to take.

Thus it was that, a little while later, I stepped out of the hotel entrance into a bright if rather chilly morning that required me to button up my coat and summon a carriage to take me to the British Embassy. I was feeling, at last, as though our assignment had begun in earnest.

MEETING THE AMBASSADOR

I found the Embassy to be rather busy when I arrived, but my visit was expected and I was quickly given entry and shown through to a large and finely furnished room at the rear of the building overlooking a small garden. A minute or so later, a member of staff arrived to lead me through to the Ambassador's office.

Sir George Spence was a short, thin man who wore rather thick spectacles and spoke with something of a lisp. His secretary had warned me not to draw attention to this, as the Ambassador had worked hard to overcome it and found it dispiriting whenever it was mentioned. The Spence family had, I knew, made their fortune trading fine silks from India during the last decade of the eighteenth century and Sir George's home in England was a fine Palladian affair on the Wiltshire and Dorsetshire border.

Sir George welcomed me with a firm handshake and led the way to a pair of elaborately decorated chairs placed either side of an enormous fireplace; which, fortunately, was not lit. He moved quickly and decisively, a man brimming over with energy, and there was a shrewd, observant look in his eye. I was left with the impression of a man well-equipped for the never-ending demands of his role.

"It's good to meet you, Templeman. We have, of course, been expecting you and my senior staff and I were comprehensively briefed as to your mission, a rather important one, I must say."

He spoke in the crisp, clear, confident tones of a well-educated man, though I found his rather intense gaze a little disconcerting.

"Good of you to make time to meet me, Sir George," I replied, settling into my seat. "There are, in fact, two of us. My colleague, George Stoneman, has gone in search of a contact recommended to us by the Bureau. He sends his apologies."

"Not at all, not at all. You fellows are right to make a start as soon as you can. Can I offer you a cup of tea, or do you prefer coffee? We've a rather fine selection here."

"I'm fine, thank you, Sir George. I had more coffee than was probably good for me at breakfast."

"Very good. Now then, before we get on to other matters, there's something important I need to tell you. Just received the news a short while ago," added Sir George, leaning forward a little in his chair. "It seems the Germans have tried to pre-empt things. Offered to write off the outstanding payments on the Sultan's loan and to provide a new one on improved terms. But here's the clever bit. In return, they want free access for their navy to Erteria's sole deep-water port."

I winced at the news. "That's the last thing we want," I observed.

"Precisely," responded the Ambassador. "The good news is that, so far, the Sultan has declined to accept the offer. If I'm not mistaken, the clever fellow will be looking to see if he can't extract better terms from someone else. That's certainly what I would do if I were him."

"At least that keeps the ball in play," I suggested. "I suppose the French and Italians would have been anticipating such a move and have something of their own ready to put forward by way of a counter-proposal."

Sir George flexed his fingers. "Suggests to me the Germans aren't terribly confident about getting their way at the conference and quite right too. If I were them I would have sent my navy straight into that port and made it a fait accompli. No need for a conference and let the French and Italians do their worst trying to force them back out. I can only suppose they don't want to be the ones who start this blessed war we're all expecting."

"They might not want to start it, but they seem to be getting themselves well prepared for it," I observed.

"To be expected," responded the Ambassador, settling back into his chair. "I'm sure all the Great Powers are doing just the same. Now then, about your mission. How can we help you? And where do you intend to start? I suppose the Bureau have given you some sort of a pointer."

I was reluctant to disappoint the Ambassador, at least as far as our having been given any kind of a plan was concerned, despite our really having very little to go on. "The fellow that Stoneman has gone in search of is our starting point. He is the kind of man who is most likely to hear about the arrival of an assassin or other suspect individuals in the city. We also anticipate that the Italian agent we will be working with will have access to all the country's law enforcement apparatus, to help us locate this individual."

"Mm, it sounds to me like you've been rushed into battle with little time to prepare or equip yourselves," said Sir George, not sounding the least bit impressed.

"I can't pretend it isn't a challenge," I replied, feeling my confidence waver. "But then all our assignments have their challenges. I'm sure that once we pick up the scent we'll close in on our quarry quickly enough."

Sir George studied me for a moment and, truth be told, I found his gaze somewhat disconcerting; it felt as if he were able to read my very thoughts.

"When do you get to meet this Italian agent you're placing so much faith in?" he asked.

"We don't know. The Italians insisted their man remain

anonymous until he approaches us with an agreed code phrase. Given how little time we have available, we expect to be approached at some point this morning."

Sir George glanced up at the large clock fixed to the wall above the fireplace.

"Well, in that case, as the morning's nearly half done, I'd better not keep you here for much longer. There is, however, someone I'd like you to meet before you leave," he added, climbing to his feet. "Captain James Hannah is our security fellow. His job is to keep the Embassy safe and sound, should anyone ever attempt to launch an assault," he added, as he walked across to his desk and pressed a brass button affixed to one corner.

The door opened almost at once and his secretary stepped into the open doorway.

"Ask Captain Hannah to join us will you, Beatrice," instructed the Ambassador.

The secretary promptly showed in a tall, slim man with prominent ears and a close cropped moustache, then closed the door behind him. Hannah marched across the room to join us standing by the fireplace.

"A pleasure to meet you, Templeman," declared the Captain, offering his hand.

"Likewise," I replied.

Hannah had an iron handshake but a soft, melodic Welsh voice. The contrast was a little peculiar.

"Hannah will make himself available to help you and Stoneman in any way he can," stated Sir George. "The Bureau informed us that the two of you arrived unarmed. Is that right?"

I confirmed it was. We had not anticipated any trouble during our journey south and had thought it best not to risk drawing attention to ourselves by carrying weapons.

"I suggest Hannah provides you with a pair of revolvers from our armoury. Best not to risk finding yourselves cornered and with no means of self-defence," added Sir George in a manner that suggested his offer was not to be declined.

"Very good of you," I replied. "Though I hope it doesn't come to an armed confrontation. If things go well, we'll leave it to the Italians to make an arrest."

"You've undergone firearms training, I assume?" enquired the Captain.

I confirmed that it was a standard part of the Bureau's instruction for new agents and that regular practice was required to ensure standards did not slip.

"Excellent. If you come with me once you're finished here, I will take you to the armoury and we can select something suited to your needs," said Hannah.

I thought perhaps my meeting with the Ambassador was already at an end, but it transpired that Sir George had something more to say before I left. He addressed me in a most serious tone.

"I have to say, Templeman, that I'm not convinced the Bureau fully appreciate the nature of the situation here. The whole place is crawling with agents from all the major powers. Even those who aren't actively involved in the conference, such as the Russians and the Ottomans, have got men on the ground. There was an incident between an Ottoman and two Russian agents yesterday morning that left one of the Russians in hospital. Of course, he made up some story about having been the victim of a mugging, but that had nothing to do with it. He wouldn't have wanted the authorities to know his real game. Everyone is jockeying for position, keen to influence matters for their own benefit and to disadvantage those of their enemies. I'm not sure I've ever seen anything quite like it and I can only imagine all of this is only going to make things more difficult for you. Dangerous too."

There was a firm nod of agreement from Hannah.

"I appreciate the warning, Sir George. I must admit I had rather expected the only players in this game would be those directly involved in the conference. It is unwelcome news that the waters are being further muddied by the involvement of others."

"Well, it's best you know the full picture, or as complete a one as we can provide," said the Ambassador, glancing once more up at the clock. "Now then, best you get on with things, after Hannah has equipped you with those weapons. Best of luck, Templeman, and don't hesitate to ask for assistance if you find yourself in a tight spot."

I left the Embassy a quarter of an hour later, with a pair of revolvers and a small supply of ammunition, all tucked neatly away inside a simple leather bag, feeling unnecessarily self-conscious. I hailed a cab and instructed the driver to take me to the Cafe Cosmopolitan, hopeful that Stoneman had been able to pick up a lead that would set us on our way. Sir George was right, time was indeed in short supply.

AN AGENT BEARING NEWS

The Cafe Cosmopolitan was a fine-looking establishment, with tables and chairs covering a wide swathe of the broad pavement outside its rather ornate exterior. It hummed with dozens of conversations that ebbed and flowed amongst the throng of customers. Although the morning had warmed sufficiently for me to find it rather pleasant, and certainly altogether more agreeable than it would have been in London, the bulk of the clientele were wrapped up in coats and shawls of a type I would reach for on a typical morning in January or February.

Having surveyed the tables both inside and out twice over and not seen Stoneman, I decided to take one in the open air, in a corner that caught the best of the sun. I ordered coffee then opened the copy of The Times newspaper that I had stopped to buy on my way from the Embassy. It was a day old, due to the delay involved in sending them on from London, but I decided it would suffice to occupy me while I waited for Stoneman to arrive.

As time ticked by, my mind began to return to the news that Sir George had conveyed and I wondered if the Sultan might decide to accept the German's latest offer. If he did, what might the consequences of that be? But it was pointless to speculate on such matters and I soon returned to the newspaper, my attention caught by a piece on the developing news from Albania.

A little later, as I began to wonder what on earth could be delaying Stoneman, I noticed a finely-dressed gentleman sitting alone at a table some twenty feet away. He had a Kaiser-like moustache and a sombre appearance and, although he too appeared to be reading a newspaper, I had the distinct impression he was observing me, though I never actually caught him in the act. Was my imagination getting the better of me, I asked myself, as it had the night before, or was I right to be concerned? It was all too easy on an assignment to develop a distinct sense of paranoia.

The bell on a small, rather pretty, stone church some eighty yards or so down the road struck for eleven o'clock, its deep tolls echoing off the walls of the surrounding buildings. I folded my newspaper in a haphazard manner and slapped it down on the table. It was forty minutes since I had arrived at the cafe and I was growing more and more restless for news from my fellow agent. Surely his continuing absence could only be due to his having heard something of interest from his contact, and he was at that very moment assiduously following up?

I was about to call a waiter over to order yet more coffee when I felt a firm tap on my shoulder and a voice whispered in my ear, "I am your New Spartan, Mr Templeman."

I looked round in surprise, wondering how someone could have crept up on me so easily, and was taken aback by the face I found looking down at me.

"But it's you," I stammered, almost entirely lost for words.

"It is, indeed. A surprise, I imagine."

The sharp brown eyes that held me transfixed belonged to none other than Catherine Bachini, whose lecture I had attended in London so recently. Confusion washed over me in waves and I struggled to regain my composure.

"But... you're a woman," I blurted, unable to fashion a

more cogent response.

"Very observant of you, Mr Templeman. I do hope you will be as quick-witted in the field," came the sharp reply.

I suppose that on another occasion this may have been said with wit or even sarcasm, but, in matter of fact, Bachini appeared restless, on edge even, her face a little flushed, as though she had been hurrying. I noticed also that she was constantly observant of the world around us, her gaze shifting restlessly from one place to another as if she was in search of something or someone. It left me even more perplexed than I had been on first seeing her standing there.

"I should apologise," I said, getting to my feet. "It's just that, well, I've not yet encountered a female agent."

I knew that Sir Joshua and Eastwood had recently been discussing the possibility of the Bureau recruiting female agents but, thus far, they had not done so. Our establishment of agents, though not administrative staff, remained entirely a male one.

"Well, you have now and, if you're over the shock, shall we get on? I'm afraid I have some very bad news," added Bachini, again glancing at the scene around us.

My whole body grew instantly tense upon hearing her words and a wholly unwelcome thought rushed into my mind.

"I'm afraid I have to tell you that the body of your colleague, Mr Stoneman, was found on the Via dei Taurini thirty minutes ago. He had been stabbed, twice, in the heart. The police are of the opinion it was the work of a professional killer and we agree."

Stoneman murdered! And so soon after our arrival in the Eternal City. I was mute with shock.

"Such a brazen attack, in broad daylight and in the centre of the city," said Bachini, anger trembling in her words. "Even our worst criminals are accustomed to waiting for the cover of darkness and prefer the less well-trodden parts of the city. But we cannot remain here. I must take you to our agency's headquarters while we wait for more news of what happened. Come along. I am concerned that you are already being watched."

But I was not yet ready to go anywhere. My wits had begun to return to me and I had questions to which I wanted answers.

"The work of a professional, you say. Why don't the police think Stoneman might have been murdered by a thief?"

"Because if that was the case they would have been a very strange kind of a thief, since they left behind his wallet and his pocket-watch. No, this was the work of the people we are here to stop, of that our agency is sure."

"You mean they simply followed Stoneman, waited for an opportunity when there were unlikely to be any witnesses, then murdered him so as to hinder our efforts at finding this assassin we are searching for? A pre-emptive strike," I added, little lines forming in the skin above my eyebrows.

"It is possible," replied Bachini. "But why was Stoneman not here with you?"

"He had gone to speak to a contact; someone in the criminal underworld," I admitted. "While he did that, I reported our safe arrival to the British Ambassador. We were due to meet again here."

"Did he expect any difficulties with this contact? Might they have murdered him?" asked Bachini.

I shook my head. "No, Stoneman seemed entirely confident the man he was meeting was someone he could trust. There was no suggestion he might be walking into danger," I added, but an unfortunate realisation was dawning on me as I spoke.

"And what was the name of Stoneman's contact?"

That, I had only now realised, Stoneman had failed to tell me. It was an oversight that was sure to cause us some difficulties.

"I'm afraid to say that Stoneman didn't mention the man's name," I admitted.

Bachini pursed her lips but refrained from criticism. After

a moment's thought she spoke again. "Well, that is most unfortunate, but we really do need to leave. The longer we remain here the greater the risk we run of being intercepted ourselves. Come, we must go to headquarters."

I followed in silence as Bachini stepped swiftly in the direction of the nearest cab. Poor Stoneman, he had hardly been given the chance to get started and had died a violent and lonely death far from home. It was a desperate thought and I sought a little consolation in the fact he had chosen to remain unmarried.

But, if my mind might have had any ideas about falling into a depression, by the time we had climbed into the cab these had been entirely dispelled, replaced by a growing desire to exact revenge. If I had ever needed any motivation to succeed in my assignment, then I most surely did not now.

A NEW RELATIONSHIP FORMS

The headquarters of the Italian Secret Service was in a modest, plain building on the Via di Sant Erasmo, its frontage looking out over a small and quiet tree-lined square. I was standing at one of the tall windows looking up at the pale-blue sky, where thin wisps of clouds drifted by. A large pigeon landed on the sill, espied me then took again to the wing, sweeping down across the square.

The door of the small, high-ceilinged room opened and I looked round to see Bachini enter.

"Colonel Morelli will join us shortly," she informed me as she placed two cups of espresso on the low, rectangular table that stood at one end of the room.

I had already spoken on the telephone to Captain Hannah at the British Embassy, Sir George being otherwise engaged, and informed him of Stoneman's murder. The body was by now in the city morgue, under police guard, which seemed a little unnecessary. Bachini had offered to arrange for me to see the body, but I knew Stoneman would have nothing about his person that might connect him to his real reason for being in Rome and such a detour would take up valuable time. Instead, I agreed with Hannah that the Embassy would make arrangements for the body to be returned to the British

Isles.

Hannah had expressed some concern at my continuing alone, but I resisted his suggestion that I await the arrival of reinforcements and pointed out that I was not, in fact, operating on my own. I had now made contact with the Italian agent assigned to work with me. In any case, I added, we could not allow ourselves to be deterred so easily, especially when to do so would mean Stoneman's sacrifice had been in vain.

I was pleased to find that Bachini was as keen as I to press on with matters and she had already set wheels in motion to help us do so. As it was, we were first required to meet with the head of the Italian Secret Service, Colonel Morelli, who wished to have his say on matters before allowing us to take up the hunt. It was frustrating, but there was nothing to be done about it and so I had been brooding in silence by that window for the past quarter of an hour.

"He won't keep us long," said Bachini, handing me a cup of espresso. "Colonel Morelli is a man of relatively few words, I am pleased to say."

I took the offered coffee and managed something close to a smile.

"I do apologise. I must have appeared ungrateful," I replied. "Stoneman being killed, and so soon after our arrival, it's really been quite a blow."

"That is understandable," answered Bachini, taking a seat on a beautifully carved and decorated chair by the window. "I would be similarly upset if it had been one of my colleagues."

I picked up a second chair and placed it opposite Bachini. My mind sought out some other topic of conversation and alighted on one I was keen to explore. "I really was rather surprised when you approached me at the cafe," I began.

"Still surprised at my being a woman," cut in Bachini, smiling.

"Ah, yes, that," I replied, studying my coffee cup. "No, or, at least, not just that. I believe I would not have been quite so surprised if I had not happened to attend your lecture in London so recently. Is the role of an academic merely a cover for your work as an agent or do you, in fact, combine the two?"

"I was an academic first," replied Bachini, sounding pleased to have something else to talk about. "I studied history and archaeology at Durham University. I then worked for a while as a conservator at the British Museum, while also researching and publishing papers on ancient Greece and its Mediterranean empire; a subject I can't get enough of. That led to my receiving invitations to lecture on the subject in Britain and several other countries, something I love to do."

"Your English is almost flawless," I observed, beginning to see why this might be.

"I have an Italian father and an English mother. They met while my father was working as a diplomat at the Italian Embassy in London. I spent the first five years of my life in London and the next three in America, before my father was assigned to a new post here in Rome."

"Quite the traveller at an early age," I remarked, thinking how plain and unadventurous it made my own life appear. "So how did all that lead to your working for the Italian secret service?"

"That was a question I asked myself when I was first approached. After all, what need could an agency like this possibly have for an expert on Ancient Greece and a female one at that," she laughed.

My cheeks grew a little warmer and wondered if I might never be forgiven for my transgression. But I also recalled my own peculiar entry into the profession of secret agent and thought perhaps Bachini's might not be so odd after all.

"You are too easy to tease," she continued.

"Yes, it seems I am. But you were saying."

"The service approached me while I was working at the British Museum. I discovered that a man I spent time talking with at a dinner party some months before was a senior official here. When the service decided they wanted to recruit their first female agents, he remembered me and thought I was the kind of individual they were looking for."

"And you accepted their offer at once?" I asked. "I must admit I took some persuasion myself. I was nowhere near as certain about my suitability for the role as were my superiors at the Bureau."

"You can no doubt imagine that I was very surprised by the offer and, at first, rather suspicious. I spoke to my father about the matter and he made a few discreet enquiries using his contacts to confirm that it was genuine. After that, it was easy for me to accept. I must admit I found the whole idea most thrilling, although I understood, of course, that there were dangers involved. I am attracted to adventure and challenge and see no reason why these should be the exclusive preserve of men."

"Indeed not," I replied, increasingly impressed by Bachini's confidence.

"The service arranged for me to begin working for the Italian Ministry of Culture. That has provided me with a justification for my frequent overseas travel and allowed me to continue building relationships and gathering information. It's also had the added benefit that I have been able to continue with my research."

"And you are based in London, are you not?"

"I spend much of my time there, but I am often away elsewhere, sometimes here in Italy, sometimes in Greece and, really, anywhere else I need to be," she added, rather breezily.

I was very much enjoying finding out about my Italian colleague and would have liked to continue the conversation but at that moment the door to the room was swept open and two men walked in. The second was a plain-looking fellow, in his mid-twenties, I judged, who wore what seemed to be a constantly worried look and seemed to find it difficult to remain entirely still. The other was a different prospect entirely. Short, thin to the point of looking unwell, he was dressed in the uniform of an Italian army colonel and had the self-assured air of a man of authority. Bachini introduced him as Colonel Morelli, head of the Italian Secret Service.

"I offer my sympathy for the death of your colleague," said Morelli in heavily accented English. "A most unfortunate event."

"Indeed," I concurred.

"But not altogether a surprise," added Morelli.

The Colonel had small grey-blue eyes that studied me closely over the ridge of his large angular nose. He seemed to be appraising me, attempting to establish what sort of individual he was dealing with, which was only to be expected since he knew very little about me. In any case, I was doing the same in return, curious to assess Sir Joshua's opposite number.

"Miss Bachini says your agency does not believe Stoneman was killed by common criminals," I prompted.

"Indeed not," replied Morelli. "It does not have the hallmarks of such an assault and our police tell us their investigations find no such suspects. No, we believe the death was caused by our common enemies. Perhaps by people they paid to do their work."

Morelli gestured to his aide, who walked over to the low table, cleared away the coffee cups then laid out a large map of Rome. We gathered round it at the Colonel's prompting before he began to set out his thoughts on what had happened and where we should be focusing our efforts.

"We know of five German agents who have arrived in the city and we have them all under close watch," he began. "None of them attacked Stoneman. There are other men who have arrived and who are not welcome here. Men who make trouble wherever they go. Our police have arrested three of them and hold them in cells until the conference is completed. Most important of all, word has reached us today of an Egyptian assassin who arrived in the city two days before. He is a most talented man and very expensive. I do not think he visits Rome to go to the opera," added Morelli, without any hint of humour.

"Have we any idea where he might be staying, Colonel?"

asked Bachini.

"A man with his description was seen eating at the Restaurant Spada on the Via dei Chiavari," answered Morelli, pointing to an area on the map close to the River Tiber. "That was last night. Since then, nothing."

"Is he likely to be the assassin we seek, sir?" I asked, somewhat hopefully. We were in need of some sort of clue if we were going to make any progress.

"We know of no one else who is a bigger suspect," replied the Colonel, those blue-grey eyes staring intently at me again. "He should be the man you seek. But he is dangerous, you must understand. You will need to take care or else suffer the same fate as your friend."

"We have the police searching for this man," said Bachini. "They are visiting every hotel and lodging house in the city centre, but it's a big job and I doubt they will complete it before the conference begins tomorrow."

"And he could be staying with associates," I suggested, rubbing a hand over my chin as I studied the map.

"Bachini has a man you will speak to who maybe can help," replied the Colonel. "He is a merchant who trades in our culture, sometimes legally and sometimes illegally, though our police cannot ever prove the latter. He has friends and associates who may be able to help you find the Egyptian."

Bachini's expression betrayed her thoughts. She clearly had some reservations about dealing with this man. She saw me looking at her and there was some reluctance in her voice when she spoke. "Antonio Barbieri is not a man who can be trusted. He runs a business trading in antique furniture and paintings, but he uses this to hide his illegal dealings, selling parts of our history and culture that he should not. He has been arrested several times and always manages to find some way to avoid being made to pay for his crimes. It would be true to say that he is more slippery than an eel."

"But his illegal dealings mean he has connections that perhaps you do not?" I suggested.

"He does. I am sure the police are doing their very best to find our Egyptian, but I am certain that Barbieri knows people who will be able to find him much sooner, so long as he has not gone into deep hiding, ready to strike."

"It would be good to think that an Egyptian might stand out in a European city, but I have seen that, like London, Rome is a very cosmopolitan place where one sees many faces from all parts of the world," I said, half wishing that the conference was to have taken place somewhere else; a Nordic city, perhaps.

"You should visit Barbieri at once," Morelli instructed Bachini. "Even he will need some time to collect whatever information he can find and time is something we do not have much of."

It was clear from Morelli's tone this was not a suggestion, more a command, and Bachini interpreted his words as I had. "We will leave at once, sir, and report back here as soon as we are done with Barbieri."

The Colonel looked thoughtful for a moment, flexing his fingers at his sides. "It is the conference ball this evening, is it not?"

"Yes, sir," replied Bachini.

"You and Templeman, you are going to the ball?"

Bachini looked at me.

"I have yet to receive an invitation." I replied. "Although I had thought that perhaps the ball was not for ordinary people like me."

"Nor am I on the guest list, sir," added Bachini.

"You must go. You will get a chance to meet your opponents, or at least their masters. And you may also see the Sultan himself. There may be dealings at the ball that perhaps tell you things about the people involved. Clues for you to sniff out. I will see to it that you both receive invitations."

"Very good of you, Colonel," I replied, feeling rather pleased at the prospect of attending such a lavish event. "Though I will be in need of somewhere to hire the appropriate attire."

"I can help you with that," smiled Bachini. "I know just the place to take you."

THE FOX'S LAIR

Catherine Bachini and I were seated in a large opulently furnished room overlooking a narrow street on which many of the buildings appeared to have been built during the Renaissance, though I suspected they had undergone many modifications since then. The room was, in fact, the office of our host, Antonio Barbieri, though to describe it as such would do it a considerable disservice.

Much of the furniture was beautifully carved from the finest of woods and dressed with exquisite fabrics in rich colours. I had felt a little reluctant to take a seat for fear it might cause some minor defect to appear. Huge paintings set in vast, carved gold-encrusted frames hung on the walls. There were country vistas, portraits of long dead nobles wearing rather serious looks and one religious piece in which a knight, partially clad in gleaming armour, prayed at the foot of a church altar. Stone sculptures filled every corner and the middle portion of the floor was dressed with an enormous Ottoman rug which even an unskilled eye such as mine could see was of the very finest quality.

The overall effect was to leave you feeling as if you were visiting the town house of a wealthy and cultured member of the minor aristocracy, or perhaps an elite merchant in the days when the Italian city states were at the very height of their power and wealth.

It was, it seemed, entirely in keeping with our host, of whom Bachini had told me a little on our carriage journey there. The man she had described was a peculiar mix. Sixty-one years of age, though he didn't look it. Energetic to the point of being restless. An entertainer and teller of stories, whose confident and outgoing nature was able to put even the most nervous of people at ease; social skills he had deployed to build an enormous network of contacts amongst the great and good in the city.

Sharp-witted, with a keen eye for an opportunity and excellent organisational skills, he was, however, also capable of being ruthless in his business dealings. These were skills that he not only used to his advantage in his legitimate business, trading in furniture and paintings, but also in his illegal one, selling pieces of ancient history and culture that the government never intended should be allowed to leave the country.

Amongst his business associates he was known as the Grey Fox, on account of his grey hair and his remarkable ability to keep himself out of prison, despite his considerable illegal dealings. Bachini made it clear that he was also to be trusted as little as a fox and that we were only there to ask for his assistance because we had so few alternatives and none that were any better. She hoped to appeal to his pride as an Italian when asking for his assistance, but rather feared he might seek to take advantage of the situation and insist on a more material inducement.

As it was, when Barbieri strode into the room he was everything I had by then come to expect and I found myself not in the least bit disappointed.

A MASTER ENTERTAINER

Antonio Barbieri looked at least ten years younger than he actually was. Energy and enthusiasm radiated from him in great waves and his dark brown eyes, set beneath bushy brows, danced with a deep-seated joy of life. He was short, about five foot six, but you were left with the impression of a man who was much taller, so strongly did his personality impress itself upon you.

Smartly dressed in a flawlessly cut dark brown suit, I got glimpses, as he moved, of what I took to be a solid gold chain for a pocket watch. On the third finger of his right hand he wore a ring into which was set an impressively large ruby. A touch extravagant, perhaps, but in keeping with the man he was.

He had been informed of our visit in advance by telephone, though I suspected he had done little more than was normal for him in preparing to meet guests and he gave off every appearance of being delighted we had chosen to spend a little time with him. He took Bachini's hand and kissed it lightly.

"Miss Bachini, the most beautiful agent the Italian Secret Service employs and a talented one at that. Who would have thought such hard-nosed people would possess such fine taste," he declared, apparently as sincere as any man could ever be.

Bachini had informed me that Barbieri had spent three years living in the United States, New York to be precise, in the early 1890s, when a crackdown on crime by a new government keen to make its mark had forced him to flee Italy. Another change in government had allowed him to return. Thus it was that, upon first hearing him speak, I was only just able to stifle a smile. Though his English was good, he spoke it with a hint of a New York accent, of the sort I had once heard from a fellow guest at a dinner party in London.

"And you must be Mr Alexander Templeman," he said, turning his attention to me. "It is an honour to meet such an eminent representative of the British Empire." His handshake was firm and committed. "A man of taste and culture, I am sure, who appreciates the finer things in life, as do I," he declared with a distinct sparkle in his eye.

"I can certainly see that you enjoy the finer things in life," I replied, gesturing to the room around us.

"Ah, it is perhaps a little… excessive," he proffered. "But most of the items you see here are either cherished ones that I keep for myself or more valuable ones from amongst my stock that I prefer to keep safely here. I admit it can sometimes seem a little… self-indulgent, but then we all have our faults, do we not," he added, smiling broadly. "But, I am forgetting my manners. Allow me to get you something to drink. Wine, perhaps? Or do you prefer tea, Mr Templeman? We have that here for our English customers also."

Barbieri was a most beguiling and charming fellow and I could already see that it would be easy for him to use such skills to his benefit. I doubted that even the Pope himself could resist making a purchase from amongst Barbieri's collection should he be subjected to the merchant's persuasive charms.

"Tea would be very welcome," I replied, realising that I had not tasted it since leaving London.

Bachini opted for coffee, at which Barbieri picked up a little brass bell, decorated with the face of a monster, that sat on a side table and rang it vigorously. A servant appeared and was sent away with appropriate instructions.

"I would offer you a tour of my premises, Mr Templeman," announced Barbieri. "We have many beautiful items here, some of them at very reasonable prices. But I understand that you are here on business, of a sort, not for the purposes of pleasure," he added, looking in Bachini's direction.

"We are," she replied, as the three of us, at our host's behest, took seats around a large, ornate stone fireplace.

"So, what service is it that I can provide to my country?" asked the merchant, sounding, for the first time, somewhat serious.

"There is a conference taking place not far from here over the next few days," began Bachini. "It is to be attended by several of the Great Powers and it is important that the outcome is a successful one. If it is not, then the consequences could be most serious, for Italians but also the rest of Europe. Word has reached us that someone wishes to see the conference fail and has taken steps to make that happen."

"Someone?" interrupted Barbieri, an eyebrow raised.

Bachini looked in my direction. I tilted my head forward just enough for her to notice.

"Our friends the Germans stand to gain a great deal if the conference fails," Bachini replied. "But our own government and that of France would not be willing to stand idly by if that was the case and war could be the result."

Barbieri remained silent for a moment, contemplating what he had just heard. I thought briefly that perhaps he might be weighing up the potential impact on his business of any war, but then chastised myself for such an uncharitable thought. There was no reason the man could not be simultaneously both a criminal and a patriot.

"And the Germans have a plan for undermining the

conference?" asked Barbieri.

"They intend to assassinate our chief negotiator, the Count Villafranca, though they don't intend to do that themselves. We have reason to believe they have hired an assassin, an Egyptian, to do their work for them," answered Bachini.

"Assassins are not one of my specialities," observed Barbieri, stroking his chin with the back of one hand. "You cannot locate this assassin and would like me to find him for you, am I not right?" he asked.

I was impressed both that he homed in so quickly on our reason for being there and that he wasted no time in getting to the point. His business instincts were sharp indeed. Our conversation fell into abeyance briefly as our drinks were brought to us and it was Bachini who picked up the thread once the maid had departed.

"It is the lack of time that is such a difficulty. The conference delegates are already here, in Rome, and proceedings begin tomorrow, which means the assassin could, or even must, strike soon. We need all the help we can get."

Barbieri picked at a non-existent spec of dust on his trouser leg. "There are people I know who could, if you so desired, arrange for this threat to be put to a permanent end, if you understand me," he suggested, a little tentatively.

Bachini and I exchanged a glance before she replied. "We would prefer to take the man alive, if possible. There may be useful information we can extract from him."

Barbieri nodded. "As a good Italian, I will of course do all I can to put an end to this threat to our safety and our honour. Our guests should not be in fear of their lives when they visit us. It might, though, prove difficult, you understand, if this man is a professional and takes trouble to hide himself away."

"All the same, I imagine your contacts are likely to find him sooner than we are," answered Bachini, who appeared, for a moment, to be a little uncertain. I could not think why that might be the case.

Barbieri's smile was warm, but there was also something else about it that I struggled to put my finger on. Was there, perhaps, a history between the two of them of which I was unaware?

"I will do my very best for you and for Italy, starting at once," said the merchant, his hands outstretched, palms up. "And I will be sure to let you know immediately if I find anything."

There was a movement by the open doorway and I looked across to see a woman standing there. She was remarkably beautiful, in the way only a southern European woman can be. As short as Barbieri, with long, rich jet-black hair and deep, beguiling green eyes. She was demur, almost reluctant, it seemed, to enter the office.

"Ah, my wife, Teresa," declared Barbieri, getting to his feet. "Teresa, my dear, please join us. This is Mr Alexander Templeman, a splendid representative of the British Government and Miss Bachini from our friends at the Italian Government," announced the merchant with a flourish, as if pleased to show us off.

So, the woman was his wife. I could also hardly fail to notice that she was much younger than Barbieri, perhaps only in her mid-twenties.

She smiled at us in turn, though remained mute, as she took hold of her husband's arm.

"Her English is not so good, though I try to teach her a little," explained Barbieri, looking joyfully into his wife's eyes.

"I suspect her English is better than my Italian," I replied.

"Perhaps. Perhaps," responded our host. "But tell me, how do you like the Eternal City, Mr Templeman? Is it not the most beautiful in all the world?"

"It is truly a beautiful city," came my immediate and honest reply. "Though I must admit I have not yet seen a very great deal of it. Perhaps once my assignment here is over I may get the opportunity to spend a little time exploring before I am obliged to return to London."

"You must not restrict yourself to only the places the tourists go. There is so much more, if you know where to look. Is that not so, Miss Bachini?"

"I would be happy to show you around the city myself, Alexander," replied my fellow agent. "But that is for another time. I am afraid that, for now, we must move on. There is a lot more work for us to do before we can contemplate a sightseeing trip."

"Do not remain a stranger, Mr Templeman," pressed Barbieri with booming enthusiasm. "Before you leave for home you must return here and I will find something small and beautiful for your wife from amongst my collection. Every man's wife should be surrounded with beautiful objects, especially when they are so eternally beautiful themselves," he added, looking once more into his own wife's deep green eyes.

*

As we climbed into our carriage, Bachini glanced back at the premises we had just left.

"He will extract a price from us, when the time comes, in return for his help," she observed, an unhappy note to her words.

"I can imagine that such trade is as much a part of his business as the buying and selling of paintings and furniture," I replied, beginning to understand the unease I had sensed in Bachini during our visit.

"I would say it is the most important part of his business," she replied. "And the most valuable."

The door to the carriage was closed and we began to move away, along the old, narrow, paved street, the sound of the horses' hooves echoing off the walls of the surrounding buildings.

"His wife was very young. Mid-twenties, I thought," I prodded.

"She is his second wife. The first died some years ago, after a long illness. Barbieri has a... passion for women and a considerable reputation for engaging in affairs. It is rumoured also that he has fathered a number of illegitimate children over the years, though if he has then he has done well to keep them from prying eyes.

"Somehow I am not altogether surprised at that news," I commented. "He is a man who seems to brim over with energy and vitality, despite his age."

"You sound as if you might be jealous, Alexander," teased Bachini, laughing at my resulting discomfort. "Come. I will drop you off at your hotel, so you can rest and prepare for the ball this evening. You will need your wits about you if you are to spot any of the currents that will be swirling under the surface. They always do at these affairs, especially here in Rome."

A LAVISH AFFAIR

The Villa Carlotta is the country residence of Gabriele Carlo D'Alessandro, Count of Villafranca, the head of the Italian delegation at the international conference. He inherited the property, along with his title, upon the death of his father in 1902 and had, Bachini informed me during the course of our journey, been quick to offer it as the venue for the conference when the Italian government approached him about heading their delegation.

It is located in the Alban Hills, a low-lying cluster of volcanic hills some 12 miles to the south-east of Rome, where the property sits on the banks of Lake Albano in what, Bachini assured me, was a fabulous setting with wonderful views. I had to take her word for all of this since, by the time we arrived, evening had descended and I could make out little of the surrounding countryside.

We stepped out of our motorcar and followed a short path that led to a round ornamental pond. In the middle of the pond sat a substantial stone figure of a goddess, from which spouted an arc of water that played a delightful melody as it re-entered the pond. Beyond that was a double set of wide switch-back, balustraded stone steps that led a short way up the hillside to the Villa entrance. The light from ornate gas lamps that lined both sides of the path cast a warm, flickering glow on the scene, helping to alleviate the chill of the late evening air.

"Quite the entrance," I remarked, as Bachini and I stepped forward.

"So beautiful in the evening light," she replied, looking herself something of a goddess wearing a full-length ballgown in shades of blue and a small tiara she had borrowed from her mother.

I had been told that officially there were 220 guests at the ball, but it was expected that many of those, especially the politicians, would bring with them assistants of one kind or another who would be housed in various rooms and some of the outbuildings. It was, agreed Bachini, something of a headache when it came to security arrangements.

Most of the guests must have arrived before us since, as we entered the villa, we found the place to be a bustling, noisy press of people clearly intent on enjoying themselves. I must admit to being at first a little overwhelmed by the whole affair; I was not as used as Bachini to such events. The splendour of the setting, the beauty of the people and the extravagance of their attire, as well as the presence of so many people of great political or social significance, was a lot to take in and I felt somewhat the interloper.

Bachini must have recognised my discomfort. As we made our way across the vast entrance hall towards the ballroom, she turned and asked me, "You are not familiar with such occasions, Alexander?"

I smiled a little sheepishly. "I am afraid not. The grandest social affairs I am used to attending are weddings and all of those on very much a smaller scale than this."

She laughed. "Well, stay close and I shall make sure you come to no harm."

"Harm?" I asked, a little confused.

"Oh, yes, these events are dangerous places for a handsome young Englishman," she replied, her eyes sparkling. "There are older women at these events whose husbands do not satisfy their natural needs and so they are always looking for some suitable young man to fill the void. But stay close and they will think that you are mine for the evening," she added, laughing.

I fear I may have blushed a little. Modern women had a freedom of expression that my parents' generation would find most alarming.

*

We were in the ballroom when Bachini spotted our host, the Count of Villafranca. He was surrounded by such a press of people that she settled for pointing him out rather than attempting an introduction. In his mid-fifties, the Count was of average height, somewhat overweight, and had thinning black hair that was heavily streaked with grey. His brown eyes sat above a large nose and a square chin and he had a thick moustache that he played with continually. Whereas I would have found it an unwelcome and overpowering experience to be the centre of so much attention, the Count appeared to revel in it, clearly enjoying the conversation, the gossip and the jokes that were being shared with him.

"He is a very social animal," observed Bachini, leaning in a little closer so as to make herself more easily heard above the noise of the small orchestra and the dozens upon dozens of conversations that echoed around the ballroom. "He seems to know a good deal about practically any subject you care to raise, even the gossip from the streets, and he is always eager for conversation. But it would be a mistake to think that is all there is to him, for he is a very intelligent and astute man."

"Is he is not a member of the Italian government?" I asked, thinking, for a moment, that I had read such in my briefing notes.

"No and he never has been a politician in the formal sense. He prefers to operate on the fringes, influencing and assisting where he wishes, without the drawbacks of being an actual politician. He must prove of some use because he continues to be called upon by prime ministers, as he has done for the last twenty or so years."

"Yes, I am not sure I would want to be a politician myself," I observed. "Far too much trouble dealing with the press and the voters."

A loud roar of laughter erupted from the Count's party.

"Is he a safe pair of hands to lead the Italian delegation?" I asked.

"I would say he is," replied Bachini. "There were other candidates, I am sure, but he has done similar things before and has a flair for being able to work with even the most troublesome of individuals. Whether or not even he can be successful this time, I suppose we will have to wait and see."

I was about to ask Bachini what she thought the chances were of a successful outcome to the conference when I felt a tap on the shoulder and looked around to see Sir George Spence standing there.

"Evening, Templeman," he declared. "Quite the affair, what? Enjoying yourself, are you?"

"Good evening, Ambassador," I replied. "It is, indeed, a very impressive affair. Rather grander than the social engagements I am used to back home."

"Ah, and you, I take it, must be Templeman's Italian colleague, Miss Bachini," said Sir George, turning his attention to my companion for the evening. "A pleasure to meet you."

"Likewise, Mr Ambassador," responded Bachini. "I hope you are not being too harassed this evening by my compatriots seeking favours for their businesses or family members."

"Ah, I see you understand well how these things work. I am afraid it is the lot of people in my position to have to deal with such requests whatever the occasion. But that is what my staff are for," he added, smiling as he glanced at a tall fellow who stood behind him."

There was another burst of noise from the Count's party.

"I see the Count is enjoying himself as usual," remarked the Ambassador. "I shall have to join him shortly, but before I do, tell me, Templeman, has there been any progress in your search?"

"Nothing solid, sir. But we have availed ourselves of one of Miss Bachini's contacts who stands as much chance as anyone does of tracking down our quarry. With a fair wind we may find that by the time we have put away our breakfasts tomorrow morning there will be news to report."

"Well, let's hope so. The conference starts for real tomorrow and this assassin will need to strike soon or risk acting too late."

"Yes, quite so, sir," I replied, feeling a momentary return of the tension that the formal demands of the ball had masked.

"Well, time for me to press on. Hands to shake and conversations to be had," said Sir George. "A pleasure to meet you, Miss Bachini. You should call by the Embassy for afternoon tea sometime."

And with that the Ambassador disappeared back into the crowd heading for the Count's expanding party to continue his evening's work. I was, I realised, most fortunate to be free of such demands myself.

A SHOCKING ENCOUNTER

I had rather hoped to see something of the Sultan whilst we were at the Villa, but word reached us that upon arrival he had been escorted to a large room on the first floor, where he was entertaining selected guests at what amounted to his own private reception. Assurances had been given that he would eventually join the main body of guests at the ball, but no one could say quite when this might be. I could only hope we would still be there when he did put in an appearance.

As it was, after a time, both Bachini and I began to find the noise and the close proximity of so many people a little oppressive and so we took the opportunity to retire to one of several drawing rooms, which was less heavily populated and altogether calmer.

As we sipped champagne, Bachini began to tell me a little about her family and especially her fiance, Alessandro Meazza, the second son of an Italian industrialist based in Milan.

"We met entirely by chance at a cafe in Rome, near to my father's office. Alessandro was so handsome I simply had to make an excuse to talk to him. I think he was a little surprised at me being so forward," she added, smiling at the recollection.

"That is the modern way, I believe," I replied, somewhat uncertainly, before asking, "What line of work is he in?"

"He works for his father, managing many of the company's overseas accounts, especially those in Great Britain and the United States, which is very convenient for the two of us since it allows us to see more of each other than would otherwise be the case," she observed.

"The two of you don't mind being apart much of the time, though, I take it?" I asked, as a peal of laughter went up from a small group seated nearby.

"I sometimes think it's a good thing not to spend all your time with your intended," quipped Bachini. "What is the saying? 'Familiarity breeds contempt' I believe it goes."

"Or, 'absence makes the heart grow fonder'," I suggested.

"That's the idea. We'll settle down one day and raise a family, which will be much to my mother's relief, but for the time being I believe things suit the both of us very well."

Bachini despatched the rest of her champagne and looked a little disappointed to find her glass empty.

"Another?" I asked.

"Oh, yes please. A little extravagant, maybe, but why deny yourself when you might drop down dead tomorrow?"

"Does Alessandro not have concerns about your activities as a government agent?" I enquired, as I looked around for a waiter.

"Oh, he doesn't know," she replied, without hesitation.

"He doesn't know?" I repeated, a little taken aback.

"Certainly not. Why cause him the worry, especially when there isn't any reason for him to know? In any case, he spends so much time travelling the world that if either of us should be worried about the other then it really ought to be me. Ships do have a nasty habit of disappearing beneath the waves."

"Well, yes, I suppose there is some truth in that," I said, not sure I could have come up with a counter-argument, even if I had wanted to.

It was Bachini who spotted a waiter and while she was

exchanging her empty glass for a full one my attention was drawn to a group of four men standing together about twenty yards away. One of them, a tall fellow whose neat light-brown hair was flecked with a little grey, had his back to me and seemed to be engaged in good-humoured conversation with the other three, all of whom appeared to be somewhat deferential towards him. A waiter approached them with a tray of canapés and, as the tall man turned to take one, I got a sight of his face for the first time.

My whole body tensed in an instant and the grip I had on my champagne glass became so great that I was at risk of breaking it. The face I could now see, with its sharp features, thick moustache and penetrating brown eyes, was a familiar one and unwelcome at that, being none other than Kurt Von Luck, a leading agent in the German secret service.

"Good Lord," I gasped, barely aware I had spoken the words.

"Alex, is there something wrong?"

It was, in fact, the second time Bachini had asked the question, but I was so shocked I had not heard her the first time. She had to shake my arm in order to break the spell I was under.

"Wrong?" I asked, somewhat feebly, looking at her briefly then back at Von Luck. "I... It's...It's someone from my recent past," I finally managed to say, before bringing my attention back to her.

Her eyes narrowed a little as she peered across the room in more or less the direction I had been staring. "Who? Not someone pleasant, I am guessing. Is it one of those four men over there?"

I could see she was looking directly at Von Luck and his associates.

"Yes," I answered, feeling an uncomfortable tightness in my jaw.

"They look like Germans to me," Bachini observed. "Which one has upset you?" she asked, eagerly.

"The tall one in the middle, who the others are fawning

over," I replied, trying to let go of some of the tension I felt. "That is Kurt Von Luck, one of the German secret service's senior agents and a man who has caused much unhappiness in my life."

"That's Von Luck, is it? I've heard of him. A skilful operator, I am told, but also a ruthless one."

Bachini observed him closely. I could all but see her mind picking him apart, bit by bit, and filing it all away in her head for later use.

After a short while our scrutiny drew the attention of one of Von Luck's party and the man, a short fellow with eyes unnaturally close together, made a comment to his superior, casting a glance in our direction as he did so. Von Luck turned, looked in our direction, smiled, if I dare call it that, then said something to the others before walking across the room to join us.

"Mr Alexander Templeman, if I am not mistaken," he announced, rather formally.

"And you, I believe, are Kurt Von Luck, most recently a part of the Kaiser's diplomatic mission to Great Britain," I answered, biting back my anger and contempt.

"Quite so," he replied. "And I see you enjoy the company of a most delightful acquaintance," he added, directing his attention towards Bachini.

"Allow me to introduce you to Miss Catherine Bachini," I said, wishing my encounter with the German had taken place somewhere isolated and unobserved, so that I could give free reign to my burning desire to make the man pay over the deaths he was responsible for.

"A great pleasure to meet you, Miss Bachini," said Von Luck before giving a stiff little bow that was so excessively formal it looked absurd.

"The pleasure is mutual," replied Bachini, her manner welcoming and her voice warm. I suspected she wished to maintain a facade of rather disinterested innocence, as if she knew nothing of the man. "Are you with the German delegation to the conference? I did at first wonder if you might be a newspaper reporter who has managed to find their way into this evening's ball?" She smiled sweetly at the German, as if she might be teasing him.

"Ah, I am found out," declared Von Luck, in mock surprise. "My editor will now have to send a replacement for me." He laughed, unconvincingly. "But, no, I am indeed with the German delegation and looking forward to the start of the conference tomorrow. I hold out every confidence that we will reach an outcome that is acceptable to all parties, especially when we have such skilled negotiators as your own Count Villafranca to help things along."

His pronunciation of the Count's name was painful to hear, but Bachini was not inclined to take him to task over the matter and I decided to follow her lead.

"I am sure the Count will represent our case very effectively," Bachini replied. "Especially when it is such a strong one."

Von Luck could not resist taking the bait. "Ah, but does not the Kaiser have a strong case also? After all, the terms of our loan with the Sultan are most clear and we would be doing nothing more than claiming the agreed compensation should he not be able to make the regular payments. The wording is most unambiguous."

He was, I could see, attempting to remain good humoured, but could not altogether hide an undercurrent of arrogant superiority. I smiled inwardly, knowing there was precious little chance of the Kaiser walking away from the conference with anything more than breadcrumbs, since allowing him to take more could not be tolerated by any of the other parties involved.

"Where words are concerned, there is always room for ambiguity," responded my fellow agent and it occurred to me that Von Luck might very likely not know Bachini worked for the Italian secret service.

"I believe not in this case, Miss Bachini," re-asserted the German, his nose twitching. "But let us not come to an argument on such things tonight. The conference delegates can do that quite happily for themselves over the course of the next two days. Tonight it is for us to enjoy ourselves and is this not the most splendid of settings? I am told the gardens are quite magnificent, but sadly we cannot, of course, see them in the dark. I shall have to hope there is some time during the next two days to explore them a little."

"That is true," answered Bachini, "Though the gardens are best seen earlier in the year. Perhaps you could return another time."

"Perhaps, indeed," said Von Luck. "But for now, please allow me to make a toast to a successful conclusion to the conference and a most welcome outcome to all concerned," he declared with enthusiasm.

As he held up his champagne flute with his left hand I could see the foreshortened little finger, the tip of which he had reportedly lost in an accident whilst training with the army. I couldn't stop myself from wishing that it had been his head that had been sliced off rather than a finger tip.

"Quite so," I replied with mock enthusiasm of my own as I raised my glass.

"I'm sure there can't possibly be any other outcome," chimed in Bachini, brightly, though I thought there was perhaps an edge to her voice that carried another meaning. If there was, then Von Luck showed no sign of having noticed.

"Well, I must not allow myself the pleasure of spending all of the evening in your company, Miss Bachini, tempting though that is. And likewise yourself, Mr Templeman. It is the lot of the diplomat to spend his time toadying to those he might wish to exercise some influence over at a future date and there are a great many such people here this evening. It was a pleasure to make your acquaintance, Miss Bachini, and I do hope we have the opportunity to meet again before the conference is over."

Von Luck gave another stiff little bow to Bachini before turning on his heels and walking back to his colleagues with the measured military gait I was familiar with. I bristled with frustration at having been obliged to be civil towards the man and felt a compelling need to vacate the room.

"It's begun to feel exceedingly stuffy in here," I remarked, in a somewhat bad tempered manner. "Perhaps we can find somewhere cooler, where the company is not so offensive."

Bachini eyed me for a moment before replying, "There is a large terrace outside. I'm sure we will find it considerably cooler there."

DARKNESS DESCENDS

We made our way outside, on to a broad balustraded stone terrace that was lit by the same type of gas lamps we had passed on our way up to the villa entrance. The evening had begun to feel a little cool, but the terrace had the undeniable advantage of not only being well away from Von Luck and his cronies but also from other people. There was a single group of four engaged in conversation, but we simply went to the opposite end of the terrace to ensure our privacy.

Lights from a handful of other buildings were dotted across the hillside and there was the unmistakable scent of a late-flowering jasmine on the air. Somewhere out beyond the terrace was a large garden, but in the darkness its secrets remained hidden from my searching eyes. I took a deep breath, held the cool air in my lungs for a moment, then allowed it to seep slowly out, a little of the tension in my body easing out with it.

"An interesting man," observed Bachini.

She had no need to refer to Von Luck by name. I knew at once who she was talking about.

"I suppose that's one way of describing him," I replied, a degree of bitterness in my voice.

"Though not as impressive on first meeting as I had

expected," continued Bachini, leaning on the balustrade as if looking over the gardens. "He seemed rather arrogant. Too much so for someone in his line of work. Arrogance leads to mistakes."

"I certainly agree he is arrogant, but don't allow that to tempt you into thinking he isn't dangerous, because he's both skilful and ruthless. I for one should know that."

Bachini turned to face me once more. "You said he has killed people. Can you tell me who?"

I fiddled a little with my collar before leaning on the balustrade alongside Bachini.

"One man he ran through himself in London, using a sword concealed in a walking cane. I was following him at the time and only lost track of him temporarily, but it was long enough for Von Luck to complete his business. It was an entirely needless killing. Brutal and pointless. The other victim was a scientist I was tasked with taking care of. On that occasion, Von Luck sent his men to do the job and they would have done for me too if not for some small display of skill on my part and a generous portion of luck." I took a breath before adding, "As I said, he is both skilful and dangerous and not to be underestimated."

Bachini contemplated what I had said before asking a question I had already asked myself. "Do you think he may have arranged for the murder of Stoneman?"

I felt the skin on my forehead tighten a little. "Knowing now that Von Luck is here, then, yes, I believe it is entirely possible he arranged for Stoneman to be eliminated. I still don't know who Stoneman went off to speak to, but he seemed pretty confident of finding out something useful."

"So, Von Luck might have acted to protect his assassin?" questioned Bachini.

I nodded. "Precisely. He's not the sort of man to leave anything to chance."

We stood in silence for a time, both of us looking into the darkness, deep in thought. Von Luck's presence had changed the picture considerably for me and it seemed Bachini was also beginning to realise the significance of this new development.

It was Bachini who eventually broke the silence. "Perhaps Colonel Morelli can arrange for him to spend the weekend in a police cell. I'm sure we can come up with some supposed justification for his arrest and all we would need to do come Monday morning is announce we have proved his innocence and give him back his freedom."

"I would be delighted if that were possible," I replied, before adding with reluctance, "but I fear Von Luck would simply produce his diplomatic credentials and claim immunity from any such incarceration, more's the pity. It would be amusing to think of him being locked in a tiny cell with some brute of a fellow who has been arrested after downing far too many beers."

"Yes, I suppose you are right. But I will speak to Colonel Morelli, as he may want to have Von Luck followed whenever he leaves his hotel."

I cast my mind back to the days I spent following Von Luck in London. He was not an altogether easy man to follow, more than capable of throwing off a pursuer. But that was for Morelli and his men to deal with, if he should choose to have the German agent put under observation. I turned my thoughts to other matters.

"I can't help but wonder if Von Luck's confident assurance the Kaiser will get his way was down to something more than the terms of their loan to the Sultan. It makes me feel certain we absolutely must find this assassin as quickly as possible. Heaven knows what will happen if he is successful," I added.

"We shall begin our hunt again in the morning. Early," replied Bachini. "And, if we are fortunate, perhaps we might wake to find that Barbieri has news for us. He is a most efficient operator."

A dozen or more people, noisily engaged in several simultaneous conversations, spilled out on to the terrace, sequinned ball gowns and gem-encrusted necklaces sparkling in the gas light. A female voice expressed disappointment at the Sultan's failure to mingle with the crowd; it was easy to imagine there was a good deal of interest in the central figure of the conference amongst the ball guests and that many others were equally frustrated at the Sultan's preference to remain out of sight.

This brought an end to the peace and quiet Bachini and I had enjoyed and was the prompt for us to return inside. However, before we did so we agreed that we would depart within the hour and make an early resumption of our pursuit of the assassin the following morning. Matters were becoming critical and the prospect of failure loomed ever larger.

WELCOME NEWS

I awoke before six the following morning, after a fitful night's sleep, my mind plagued by recollections of my previous encounters with Von Luck and the potential implications of his presence in Rome. As I pulled back one set of curtains, sunlight flooded into the room and warmed my skin. Was it perhaps a harbinger of a better day ahead? It would have been nice to think so, but I had never been one to believe in such nonsense and this was no time to change my mindset. All the same, I found myself in good spirits as I washed and dressed, despite my tiredness. By the time I left my room I was very much looking forward to a good breakfast before Bachini arrived to collect me.

The restaurant was sparsely populated when I entered it a little before seven. A rotund woman with an extravagant mass of grey hair piled on the top of her head sat opposite her bald, bespectacled husband by one of the tall windows. They ate slowly, seemingly with little interest, and in silence. In the far corner, a tall, narrow man sporting quite the most absurdly long, thin moustache was reading his newspaper, a coffee cup held, immobile, in one hand, as if he feared to move it. Something he read amused him and he chuckled quietly to himself, still without moving the coffee cup.

There were a half a dozen other tables in use, but at that point a smartly-dressed waiter appeared and escorted me to a table towards the middle of the room. I ordered coffee and toast, along with kippers, eggs and mushrooms. The Italian mushrooms used by the hotel chef were, I had already discovered, remarkably good; strongly flavoured and full-bodied. As I waited to gorge myself on this splendid feast, I opened my copy of The Times to see what events back home I had been missing and what, if any, early expectations there were of the conference that was about to begin.

It was some thirty minutes later when the waiter returned to my table carrying a small envelope on a silver tray. My breakfast things had already been cleared and I was enjoying a third cup of coffee as I perused the last few pages of my newspaper.

"A message, sir," announced the waiter. "Received by telephone a short while ago."

I took up the proffered envelope and thanked the man. My curiosity was considerable, since I had no expectation of receiving any messages at that time. It had been sent by Bachini and what was written on the single sheet of paper was brief and to the point. Barbieri had been in touch with her already that morning to say he believed he may have discovered the man we were looking for. Bachini signed off by saying she would be arriving to collect me at once.

I felt a jolt of excitement run through me. Could it really be so? Had Barbieri's associates found the assassin so soon? What a relief that would be. I smiled. If this was indeed the assassin then his removal from the scene would change matters at the conference entirely, not only in saving the life of an Italian count. Such a development would wipe away Von Luck's arrogance. I only wished I could be there to see the look on his face when the news was broken to him.

*

Bachini arrived less than ten minutes later and we were at once on our way across the city in a chauffeur driven motorcar. Her excitement was palpable as my own.

"It will be quite the relief if this is indeed our man," I said, having to raise my voice to be heard above the noise of the engine.

"Absolutely. Morelli has insisted on strengthening the Count's security arrangements, but there is only so much that can be done. It will be much the better if we have this assassin under lock and key," replied Bachini, holding on tightly as the motorcar navigated a sharp bend at a little more speed than was prudent.

"The driver is eager," I observed.

Bachini smiled. "I told him to drive quickly. He clearly took me at my word."

Some fifteen minutes later we came to a halt at the entrance to a narrow, cobbled street. The stone and brick buildings along either side seemed to lean in disconcertingly; so much so that it was a wonder they didn't meet at the top. Most had seen better days, paint flaking away from timber and tiles missing from rooftops. The strong aroma of coffee did battle with a more general smell of decay and poverty.

"It is a poor area," pointed out Bachini as we looked through the window. "There are many inexpensive boarding houses in places like this where a man could hide away with no one intruding on his privacy. Money is good at buying silence in such a place."

"Let's hope Barbieri's money is of more value," I replied, leaning forward to get a better look along the street.

As I did so, a short, thin youth, who could have been no older than fifteen or maybe sixteen, appeared by the window with the nervous, shifting look of someone who was always on the look out for signs of danger. He gestured to us to join him.

"He must be Barbieri's man," said Bachini. "He will show us which boarding house the Egyptian is in."

Bachini exchanged a few words in Italian with the youth,

who pointed towards one of the buildings on the left side of the street and said something more.

My fellow agent turned to me and explained, "The Egyptian is in the boarding house with the blue door." When I nodded to confirm I had picked it out she continued. "He has not left the building since going out for something to eat earlier this morning and, according to this young man, he is in the rear room on the second floor."

"Is he alone?" I asked.

Bachini spoke to the youth again before answering. "Yes, he has been alone since they located him late last night."

"That was quick work. But what makes them so sure he is our assassin? There must be other Egyptians staying in the city?" I enquired.

There was another exchange between Bachini and Barbieri's man before she turned back to me. "Barbieri's informants were very clear who this man is and, just to be sure, our friend here slipped into the Egyptian's room while he was out earlier and found a rifle wrapped in a sheet hidden behind a cupboard. It does sound as if he is the man we are looking for," she added, glancing back at the building with the blue door.

I happily concurred.

"Are you armed?" asked Bachini, as she slipped a small revolver from a pocket in her long, black coat.

I was momentarily taken aback, seeing her handle the weapon with a practised ease as she satisfied herself all was in order. Patting a somewhat bulging pocket in my jacket I confirmed I was indeed armed with a revolver of my own, now very thankful for Captain's Hannah's loan from his small armoury.

It was strange, but, at that moment, with my senses suddenly so much more heightened, I began to notice the world around me with an altogether sharper eye. The middle-aged, dark-haired woman, smoking a cigarette as she leaned on the edge of her first-floor balcony, who seemed unable to take her eyes off a much younger man labouring to repair a broken door on a building opposite. Two young boys, perhaps three or four years of age, dressed in clothes that were little more than rags, whose bare feet skipped lightly across the cobbles as they chased a most forgiving cat. The intermingling smells of cooking, coffee and freshly laundered clothes on short lines hung here and there above the streets. And the irregular sounds that echoed up from the wheels of passing carts as they made their way along the cobbled street.

But I was rudely brought back to earth by a painful jab in the ribs from Bachini. Before I even had time to object to her violence, she was pushing me towards the rear of the motorcar.

"Faster, you fool," she whispered, her voice edged with concern.

We had been about to make our way down the side of the street, led by Barbieri's man, towards the lodging house. But before we had taken our first step the picture had changed entirely. As we peered with caution around the side of the motorcar, I caught sight of a tall dark-skinned man as he walked with a long easy stride away from us, down the cobbled street we had been about to enter. Dressed in a rather smart dark-blue suit and carrying a long, slender cane, he looked incongruous in such a deprived area of the city.

Barbieri's man pointed rather excitedly and Bachini whispered in my ear that the man who had just left the lodging house we were intent on was, in fact, the Egyptian assassin.

"He is very finely dressed," observed my fellow agent, her curiosity clearly piqued as much as was mine.

"It does seem a little odd," I replied. "Especially if he is seeking to maintain a low profile in such a poor area of the city."

Bachini's eyes narrowed a little. "I wonder if he might be dressed like that because he is on his way to the Villa Carlotta?"

"But he doesn't appear to be carrying his rifle," I suggested.

"Perhaps that is not his only weapon. He may have one already hidden away close to the villa. We must follow him," insisted Bachini, immediately stepping out from behind the motorcar. "Come on, Alexander, or he will get away," she commanded, as I hesitated.

As I stepped forward, Bachini spoke briefly to Barbieri's man, who nodded once, then turned on his heels and departed.

"We have no more need of him," explained Bachini. "We've found the man we've been looking for and all we need to do now is make sure he doesn't get an opportunity to take the Count's life."

There was something close to a thrill of excitement in her eyes and, I must admit, I felt the same emotion myself. Now, after being so convinced we were never going to find the assassin and that I would be forced to return to London alone and an unmitigated failure, we were closing in on our quarry. As we made our way along the cobbled street, my body tingled with the thrill of the chase and the anticipation of the confrontation that was to follow.

A PURSUIT, AT LAST

The Egyptian moved deceptively quickly and we almost lost track of him from the first, as he reached the far end of the street and turned left into a small courtyard, around which narrow stone buildings clustered tightly, as if fearful of being alone. There were three streets leading off the courtyard and we were only just in time to see which one the assassin took. We quickened our pace as we followed.

Bachini and I had agreed, as we made our way past the lodging house, that we would, initially at least, try to undertake our pursuit without being seen by the Egyptian. It was possible he might be on his way to meet with collaborators in advance of continuing on to the Villa Carlotta and it would suit our cause all the more to ensure we collected up any such individuals.

This, however, made our task altogether more difficult since, as anyone who has engaged in such a pursuit will be aware, it requires no little skill to simultaneously keep your quarry in sight and avoid detection. Hold back too far and you risk losing the person you are following. Be too bold and you are almost certain to be seen. When they are moving as quickly as the Egyptian, it makes things more difficult still.

As a result, I began to feel a degree of nervousness, in

addition to the thrill of the chase, as my mind began to question where the man might be heading and for how long we would need to maintain the pursuit. Bachini remained silent, her attention seemingly fixed entirely on our quarry. If she too was beginning to feel at all nervous then she certainly wasn't displaying any signs of it.

After several worrisome minutes the Egyptian stopped abruptly outside a milliner's and we just managed to duck behind the cover of a stall selling fruit and vegetables. I wondered what on earth the man could want with a milliner, as we peered cautiously around the side of the stall. However, it transpired it was the tobacconists next door he was intent on and we watched him disappear inside.

Bachini and I had begun to debate whether or not the tobacconists might be a convenient rendezvous for our quarry to meet an accomplice when the man promptly reappeared in the street. He stopped a few yards further on, in the lee of an empty building, and proceeded to light up a pipe that he produced from a pocket in his jacket. He was most precise in his movements and fastidious about his business. After taking a few draws on the pipe, to satisfy himself the job had been well done, he continued on his way, strolling at a more regular pace now, savouring his tobacco.

After a further several minutes, during which time the Egyptian had paused to peruse the goods on offer in several shops, he came to a large courtyard where a fine old oak gave shelter to a wooden bench. At the entrance to the courtyard, a bedraggled beggar sought alms and our quarry stopped to give the man a few coins. That done, he continued to the bench and sat down, still smoking his pipe. He looked for all the world as if he was out for nothing more than a morning's walk and a chance to enjoy his pipe. It certainly was not, Bachini agreed, the behaviour of a man intent on assassinating a leading delegate at an international conference. Perplexing was the word that lingered in my mind.

By good fortune, there was a small cafe in one corner of

the courtyard and Bachini and I were able to reach this by passing behind the Egyptian. We took a table at the window and ordered coffee.

"The man shows absolutely no sense of urgency," I remarked with some frustration, as I studied the back of the so-called assassin's head.

"I would be very surprised if Barbieri has got things wrong," replied Bachini, but little wrinkles of doubt appeared on her forehead. "In his line of illicit business, making a mistake about such things can sometimes end up with you losing a lot more than mere money."

"But what is he doing here?" I asked, tapping my fingers on the table in annoyance. "You think he might be meeting someone?"

The large, chubby-faced woman who had welcomed us to the cafe returned with our coffee and Bachini said something to her which caused her to look through the window. More words were spoken before the woman returned to her station.

"I asked her if she had ever seen the man sitting on the bench before and she said she had. He was there at the same time yesterday," said my colleague, with a most satisfied look on her face.

I straightened up in my chair at once.

"And another man arrived shortly after," added Bachini. "Unfortunately, the woman didn't see anything more of them."

"So it is a rendezvous spot," I exclaimed, relieved to hear we were not, it seemed, on a wild goose chase after all.

It was, in fact, less than three minutes later when a short, wiry man with a bald head and a vast beard walked into the courtyard in a hurry and went straight over to the Egyptian, who promptly brought out his pocket-watch. and held it up for the other man to see. It was clear enough the new arrival was late. There was a brief exchange between the two before the Egyptian stood up and they began to walk across the courtyard in the direction of one of the exits. Bachini and I were on our way out of the cafe at once.

By this time, I had absolutely no idea where I was, being almost entirely ignorant of the city's layout. We could have been practically anywhere, north, east, south or west. But one thing that remained consistent was our continuing presence in what must have been one of the poorer areas of the capital city. By turns, it provided an atmosphere that was either brooding, oppressive, or deeply disheartening. I was later to learn from Bachini that it also harboured a good deal of the criminal element of the city, which no doubt was an attraction to the man we were following.

We had gone only some three hundred yards when the two men ahead of us disappeared into what we found to be a narrow, damp alleyway where the buildings closed in so tightly that they brought an unwelcome gloom to the place. The footsteps of the two men echoed off the stone walls, causing us to hesitate at the alley entrance for fear of giving ourselves away. We moved forward only after we observed the Egyptian and his colleague enter a building on the right.

The doorway through which we peered opened up into a dark hallway. The unpleasant smell of damp and decay was heavy on the air and it was so chilly in the narrow, low-ceilinged space that I shivered. As my eyes adjusted to the low level of light I could see the place was in a most dilapidated state, paint flaking from woodwork, sections of plaster hanging from the ceiling and rubbish of all sorts collected in corners.

As we wondered where our quarry had gone, there came the sound of squeaking floorboards from the stairwell to our left, followed by the murmur of a man's voice. Bachini and I exchanged a glance and produced our revolvers before I placed a foot, most tentatively, on the first tread of the stairs, my heart rate beginning to quicken.

By the time we reached the top of the stairs, my palms and temples were somewhat sweaty and my breathing a little shallow. The voices of what appeared to be three men could now clearly be heard in a room at the end of a short landing.

A few moments more and we would be right on top of them. A confrontation loomed large and my feelings swung violently from excitement to fear and back again.

Bachini too appeared tense, little lines etched on her forehead and the glint of perspiration coming from her temples. I had not asked her beforehand if she had any experience of such a potentially violent encounter and I wondered if it might not be best for her to stay back as I went forward. But she clearly had no such intention and began to edge forward, keeping her body low.

As we peered in through the narrow gap between the door and its frame, we found ourselves looking upon a large room moderately well lit by a pair of windows in the opposite wall. The room was empty save for a large, battered table, around which stood the Egyptian and two other men. The object of their attention was what I took to be a fine example of a sniper's rifle that lay on the table, along with a small collection of supporting equipment.

I felt a hand settle on my shoulder and looked across to see Bachini gesturing for us to head back the way we had come. I shook my head and pointed my revolver at the room before us, but Bachini gestured again, more insistently this time, towards the stairs. With considerable reluctance I followed her back along the hallway.

"We should take these three men alive, if we can," whispered my colleague as we stopped outside the doorway to the property. "If we can extract the truth from them under interrogation, it will surely put an end to any hopes the Germans have of obtaining a favourable outcome from the conference."

"It would cause something of an international confrontation if they owned up to being paid by the Germans to assassinate Count Villafranca," I replied, wiping a little sweat from my forehead. "But why bring us back down here? With the element of surprise on our side, we could surely have captured those men."

"We might be able to or we might not," responded

Bachini. "Remember, they have a professional assassin amongst their number and... well, I have no experience of this sort of thing. I wouldn't want to let you down."

It was the first time I had seen any lack of confidence on the part of the Italian agent and I suspected it irked her to have to admit as much. But, I had to remind myself, she had made it clear before what sort of work she did for the Italian Secret Service and that did not include gun battles with desperate enemy agents or their allies. I also recalled my own first such encounter, terrifying as it was, and felt nothing but respect for her actions.

"There is a police station a short distance from here," she continued. "My suggestion is that I bring back reinforcements from there, so those men upstairs have no option other than to surrender. If you wait here, in case the Egyptian leaves before I return, you will be able to continue following him."

"That is an entirely sensible plan," I agreed. "At the very least, we will still end up with the Egyptian in our sights. But you'd best be quick about it, because I'd much prefer to take all three of them."

A CONFRONTATION ERUPTS

I must have checked my pocket-watch. more than a dozen times as I loitered in that damp, gloomy doorway, fearing that at any moment I would hear the tread of footsteps as the three men began to descend the stairs. I wondered whether or not I ought to attempt to block their way should they try to leave before my colleague returned. Three guns against one was a daunting prospect, but perhaps I could reduce their numbers by one before they had a chance to respond. All the same, these men were professionals and not to be taken lightly. Failure on my part would risk the Egyptian making good his escape and the consequences of that would likely be disastrous.

In matter of fact, Bachini returned, in company with four members of Rome's police force, barely more than eleven minutes later. My expectations of a positive outcome surged as I watched their near silent approach, certain we now had the numbers to overwhelm our foes, especially if we could retain the element of surprise.

With Bachini acting as interpreter, we reached an agreement with the senior police officer that the best option was to lie in wait for the three men upstairs to descend, then overwhelm them. It offered the least likelihood of danger to us, while also presenting us with an excellent chance of success. With that agreed we took up positions, some of us hiding inside the building and two of the police officers tucked into the doorways of neighbouring buildings.

The morning had all but passed and from a nearby church I heard the bells strike for a quarter-to-twelve as I stood rigid as a board behind a door that hung precariously on one hinge, my revolver in one hand, poised to leap into the hallway. But time continued to tick by and still there was no sign of the three men. I began to feel increasingly uneasy, wondering if there could possibly be some other exit that Bachini and I had failed to spot. Surely our adversaries had completed their business by now.

Bachini was clearly beginning to have the same concerns, for she removed herself from her own hiding place and made her way along to the room I was hiding in.

"Are you thinking there may be another way out of here?" I asked, at a whisper.

"I didn't see any," she replied, leaning in close. "But perhaps there is. Surely they should have come back down by now?"

I nodded, my lips pursed. "Perhaps we ought to take the initiative and head upstairs," I suggested, fairly certain now that was precisely what we should do.

I never did get to find out what Bachini's own thoughts on the matter were for, at that moment, my ears were filled with the violent, ringing explosion of a gun, followed at once by a cacophony of shouting and an eruption of weapons being fired.

It took me a moment to regain my senses before peering, with considerable care, into the hallway. One of the police officers rushed by, shouting something I could not understand. Another was on the bottom step, his eyes wide, as he fired up into the stairwell like someone possessed. His colleague took his arm and shook him before the two of them were forced to jump aside as a series of bullets thudded into the wall beside them.

Bachini and I stepped into the hallway, our backs pressed against the wall, just as one of the officers went to run up the stairs. He immediately let out a howl of pain as a bullet passed through his right thigh and he fell to the ground. His colleague let off a flurry of shots as the injured man dragged himself out of the line of fire, his face etched with pain.

By now the two officers who had been waiting outside were at the open doorway and, acting upon a signal from the other, they laid down a volley of covering fire as he rushed up the uneven steps. I wasted no time and immediately followed him, veering from one side to other so as to make myself a more difficult target.

The weight of the fire from below did its trick, forcing the villains to retreat from their vantage point, deeper into the house. As we reached the top of the stairs, the officer and I were able to tumble through an open doorway into a small room on the far side of the landing while bullets thudded into the plaster and woodwork all around us.

My heart was racing and I was breathing heavily but, benefiting from my previous experience of such situations, I found that I was increasingly in control of my senses and I began to weigh up our situation. The Egyptian and his two associates were in the large room at the end of the hallway. They could, if they wished to risk it, perhaps jump out of a window, but a fall from the first floor might result in broken bones and I judged they would not yet be ready to resort to such measures, no doubt confident in their ability to gain the upper hand. After all, they had a professional assassin amongst their number.

The police officers, however, were in no mood to be bested, nor even put on the back foot and, as the man alongside me laid down covering fire, the other two rushed into the room opposite. We were now in a position to fire upon our enemies from both flanks and, as soon as one of them leaned out from behind cover to fire off a couple of shots at the officers in the other room, I let off two shots and took satisfaction in seeing him slump forward onto the floor, motionless.

For a moment there was silence, both sides requiring a little time to assess the new situation. I reloaded my revolver and snapped it shut as the officers exchanged a series of hand gestures. They seemed to be satisfied they had come up with an acceptable plan and the man alongside me gestured that he was going to advance and the rest of us were to provide covering fire. I wasn't sure this was wise, but had to admire the fellow's bravery. In any case, being unable to speak Italian, I had no effective way of debating with him the merits of this plan.

However, as we all set ourselves ready for the assault, pandemonium erupted in the room ahead of us. From somewhere else, bullets were ripping through the air and we watched as the second of the Egyptian's associates tumbled across the doorway and fell to the floor in a tangled heap, his revolver firing into the ceiling. Realising Bachini was nowhere to be seen, I concluded that she had managed to find some other vantage point that gave her sight of our enemies. Surely now the position was hopeless for the assassin. He must have no choice other than to give himself up.

Indeed, it seemed he quickly realised the impossible nature of his situation. However, rather than surrender meekly, he decided to make one last bid for freedom. Rushing out of the door, he laid down a ferocious burst of fire from a pair of revolvers as he surged towards the stairs. His ability to fire accurately at both us and the officers opposite under such desperate conditions was admirable, but he couldn't really have hoped to force his way through. As I took aim myself, the officer next to me fired three bullets in rapid succession, each of which hit its target. With a low guttural growl, the Egyptian stopped, tottered, let go his weapons then slipped to the floor.

I stepped forward at once and looked down at the man. He lay still and silent, with his open eyes looking up at the ceiling. Abandoned on the bare floorboards next to him was his recently acquired pouch of tobacco. Crouching down, I searched for a pulse, but there was none. Our assassin had fired his last shots and Count Villafranca could rest easy, at least for the time being.

*

As two of the officers searched the three dead men and one attended to his injured colleague, Bachini returned to the building. While we had been engaged in pinning down the assassin and his associates, she had possessed the presence of mind to cross the alleyway, enter another building and make her way up to a room opposite that gave her a clear sight of them. The explosion of fire that had caused such panic had come from her. It was an impressive performance, especially coming from someone with no experience of gun fights.

She looked exhilarated, her eyes wide and cheeks flushed as she rushed along the landing.

"Oh no, I had hoped the Egyptian would give himself up," she said, looking down at his dead body in disappointment.

"I'm not sure whether he really thought he would be able to force his way through or if he had decided not to be taken alive," I replied, as disappointed as my colleague that we had not been given the chance to interrogate him. "I suspect it was the latter."

"Well, at least we've put an end to Von Luck's plans. Perhaps we should find him and give him the news ourselves. I'd love to see the expression on his face," she added, a mischievous sparkle in her eyes.

I was about to say that was an excellent idea when I noticed a growing patch of red on the upper sleeve of her left arm.

"You've been hit," I said, pointing towards the wound.

Bachini looked at her arm then brought up a hand to prod at it. When she looked at me again she had gone a little

95

pale.

"Oh dear, you're right," she replied, in a somewhat uncertain voice. "I think I had better sit down."

THE AFTERMATH

As I escorted Bachini down the stairs, the sound of voices and running feet came from outside and soon we found ourselves mingling with new faces, further reinforcements that had been despatched by the head of police. Almost to a man, their initial looks of excitement and anticipation were replaced by ones of disappointment when they ascertained the gunfight was over.

A doctor soon appeared from out of the crowd of new arrivals and, seeing the blood on Bachini's sleeve, he promptly set about attending to her wound, which, I was relieved to hear, proved to be nothing to be alarmed about. It appeared a bullet had grazed her skin and all the treatment that was required was a little ointment and a bandage. I could swear my colleague looked disappointed it was not more serious.

The doctor was placing his equipment back in his bag and conveying some instructions to Bachini when Colonel Morelli strode up.

"You've been wounded, Bachini," he said. "Nothing serious, I hope."

"Only a graze, the doctor tells me," replied Bachini, glancing at her newly bandaged arm.

"Good. And what about our friend the Egyptian?" Morelli asked, his voice heavy with expectation.

"Dead, sir," I answered. "He and two associates."

"Ah, a shame he didn't choose to give himself up," observed Morelli, a hint of disappointment in his voice. "I would have liked to ask him a few questions. But you are sure he was our assassin, not some other Egyptian up to no good?"

I nodded. "He came here to pick up a sniper's rifle. It's in one of the upstairs rooms."

Morelli licked his lips. "And the other two men you mentioned, do we know anything about them?"

"They appear to have been couriers, here to provide the Egyptian with his rifle," answered Bachini.

"Well, it's a job well done by the both of you," said the Colonel. "The conference began as planned this morning and now we can proceed, with this threat to Count Villafranca's life having been removed. We will, all the same, maintain a heavy guard on him in case our enemies have back-up arrangements in place."

"You think that likely?" I asked, a little alarmed at the prospect.

"We have heard nothing of any such arrangements," Morelli replied, beckoning forward his adjutant. "But it is best not to take such things for granted."

He said something to the young man, who turned and stepped off smartly down the alleyway.

"The minister will want to hear the good news as soon as possible," explained Morelli. "Now then, the two of you have earned some rest, though I will, of course, being expecting your report, Bachini."

"Of course, sir."

"Perhaps now you can spend a little time exploring our fine city as a tourist," continued the Colonel, directing his attention back to me. "There is a very great deal to see and not all of it is as rundown as this street. Perhaps Bachini can draw you up a list of the best places to visit."

"I would very much like to spend some time exploring the city," I answered. "Though that will depend on Sir Joshua. He may have other plans for me."

THE BRITISH EMBASSY

Bachini dropped me off at my hotel before continuing on to the Italian Secret Service's headquarters. She had offered to take me back to the Villa Carlotta, so that I could see it in daylight, but both of us first wanted to clean up and change our clothes. Bachini was also keen to submit her report of our encounter with the Egyptian. Colonel Morelli was not, apparently, a man who looked kindly on those who kept him waiting.

As the motor-vehicle made its way down the road, I stood outside the hotel entrance and looked across the street at the parkland opposite that had seemed so brooding and menacing in the darkness of the night. Now, as it bathed in the early afternoon sunlight and with birds flitting from one tree branch to another, it offered a warm, friendly welcome and I thought perhaps I ought to pay it a visit before leaving for home.

But that would have to wait. I needed to freshen up before Bachini returned. Turning on my heels, I stepped towards the hotel entrance. But, as I did so, that familiar and unsettling sensation of being watched returned. On this occasion, however, I promptly shrugged it off. What did it matter if I was, indeed, still being observed? I had completed the task for which I had been despatched to Rome and all that remained was for me to enjoy what little time remained before the inevitable summons to return to London. I strolled into the hotel, newly unburdened of any worries and very much looking forward to a long soak in a hot bath.

*

I had one other task to carry out before Bachini collected me from the hotel and that was to pay a visit to the British Embassy, so I could update Sir George Spence on the successful conclusion of the task that had been set for me.

"Ah, Templeman," declared Sir George as I was shown into his office. "A welcome distraction from what has been a most challenging morning. How are you?" he asked, shaking my hand warmly.

"I am very well, indeed, thank you, sir," I replied as the Ambassador directed me to the same pair of chairs we had occupied on my previous visit.

"And how goes the hunt for the Egyptian assassin? The conference will be under way by now, of course," added Sir George. "Shall be travelling out to Villa Carlotta myself later this afternoon, once the preliminaries are out of the way."

"That's the very reason I am here," I answered, relaxing into the embrace of the chair. "I'm delighted to report that Bachini and I, along with a number of police officers, cornered the Egyptian and two associates a short while ago."

"Splendid news," boomed the Ambassador. "Did they come quietly or did you get to put Hannah's revolver to good use?"

"There was quite the gunfight," I replied. "Two injured on our side, while the Egyptian and his friends were all killed. It appears he intended to assassinate Count Villafanca with a sniper's rifle he collected from the building in which we cornered him."

"Sniper, eh? Yes, I can imagine the countryside around

the Villa would offer a sniper a considerable amount of cover and be rather tricky for the Italians to keep an eye on. Well, that's a splendid job, Templeman. Sir Joshua always has had a fine sense of judgement when it comes to spotting talented individuals. Shame about Stoneman, it goes without saying, but I suppose you all know the risk you are running when you sign up for the job."

"We do, indeed," I answered, immediately trying to push such thoughts from my mind.

Sir George stroked his chin as he contemplated the news I had brought him. "Wonder how the Germans will respond?" he asked, after a short while. "Easy to imagine they would have placed a great deal of reliance on their scheme being a success."

"Colonel Morelli did suggest it might be possible they have a back-up plan," I said, feeling a little unsettled by the thought. "Though he also said they have no evidence to suggest that is the case."

"Indeed. It can't be an easy thing putting such a scheme in place when the security arrangements are so considerable." Sir George looked thoughtful again before continuing, "Does make me wonder if they won't simply invade the disputed territories while the conference is on if they feel there is no hope of some sort of positive outcome for them. Deliver a fait accompli, as it were."

"Surely the other Great Powers wouldn't sit idly by while they did that?" I said, leaning forward.

"That's the problem. They wouldn't. And then where would we find ourselves? There'd be full-scale war before we knew it. Terrible thought," added the Ambassador, sounding sombre. "Absolutely terrible thought."

"Let's hope the diplomats can come up with a solution that all parties find acceptable," I proffered. "It's surprising how often they seem to be able to do just that when things have looked hopeless."

Sir George seemed to be, for a while, deep in contemplation, his gaze fixed somewhere in the space between us. He, no doubt, had access to information that someone like me did not and was, therefore, able to better judge the possibilities and likely outcomes. After a while his good mood returned and he brought his attention back to me.

"Well, I shall arrange for a coded message to be sent to London, informing them of your success," he said, before adding, "I'd ask Captain Hannah to join us, so you can give him all the gory details. He likes that sort of thing. But the fellow is off gallivanting about the countryside all day with the Italian army. Some sort of exercise or other."

I held a hand up to my head. "What a fool," I said, realising my mistake. "I'm afraid I've neglected to bring back Captain Hannah's revolver."

"Oh, that's nothing to worry about. I'm sure Hannah will be happy enough to pop over to your hotel on his return. Will give him a chance to quiz you. In any case, I think the man rather likes to get out of the Embassy whenever he can. An energetic chap like that soon finds himself feeling a little too cooped up when he has to spend any length of time locked inside four walls. His sort much prefer the outdoors world," added Sir George, before chuckling to himself.

THE VILLA CARLOTTA

I stopped for a coffee at a particularly attractive cafe on my way back to the hotel, but arrived in good time to be collected by Bachini, who appeared to have benefited as much as I from having had the opportunity to freshen up and rest a little. The drive out to the Villa Carlotta was a most pleasant one, providing me with the opportunity to take in the splendid countryside I had not been able to see on our previous visit.

Lake Albano was a fine sight, its deep, aquamarine waters sparkling in the afternoon sun. As we rounded one bend in the road I could see a little flotilla of fishing vessels, tied up at a jetty adjacent to an ancient village, bobbing gently in the wind. A little further on we passed through another sleepy village, where heavily weathered wooden shutters were closed on all the stone-built dwellings as the residents took their siesta.

The hillsides around the lake were all thick with trees and the Villa Carlotta sat in a clearing half-way up the eastern side, its marble-faced stonework bathed in sunlight. Its design was rather more plain than I had appreciated in the darkness of my previous visit, though no less attractive for that. Its four storeys were studded with small, shuttered windows that sat symmetrically either side of a more ornate middle section, the uppermost part of which included a modest balcony. The only real extravagance was the ornamental urns of an ancient design that were dotted along the front of the roof.

The Villa, Bachini informed me, had been completed between 1738 and 1763 by the Count's ancestors, who had established the estate as a way of showing off the family's new-found wealth. It had suffered somewhat at the hands of Napoleon's generals, but been restored afterwards.

As we climbed out of the motor-vehicle I looked down some steps to the right that led to the lakeside. There, alongside a stone balustraded jetty of generous proportions, two small boats with awnings that fluttered in the breeze awaited guests to enjoy a little sightseeing on the lake.

"A beautiful setting, is it not?" enquired Bachini as I stood there looking out over the lake.

"Quite wonderful," I replied. "I can see why you were keen that I see the Villa and all this during daylight," I added, sweeping a hand out before me to take in the scenery.

"If we take the path to the left at the top of the steps I will be able to show you the Villa gardens. You really wouldn't want to come all the way back out here without seeing those," said Bachini, as she turned towards the fountain and the fine set of steps we had negotiated the previous evening.

At the top of the steps Bachini spoke to a pair of soldiers standing guard at the Villa entrance before she gestured to me to follow her along a narrow path that ran down the side of the building. The path was entirely enclosed by the branches of trees that arched overhead, giving the feel of passing through a tunnel. When we emerged at the other end it was as if we had entered a brightly-lit wonderland and I stood and stared in admiration.

The gardens were remarkable. A wide expanse of lawn, with not a straight edge to be seen, ran away up and across the hillside. Surrounding this were vast borders thick with shrubs, a few of which still held on to the last of their blooms. Behind these tall, mature trees, most of which I was familiar with, were interspersed magnificent palms, some of which must have been thirty or more feet tall.

Birdsong came from all sides and here and there my attention was caught by a momentary flutter of wings. There was even a little scent still to be enjoyed from some of the plants, despite the lateness of the season.

"I can see why the Villa has such a fine reputation for its gardens," I said, still looking all around me.

"It is wonderful, isn't it," replied Bachini as she led me across the lawn towards a terrace at the back of the Villa. It must have been the one we had stepped out on to the previous evening, for I could see no other.

We had to negotiate more guards before we were allowed to enter the Villa itself. It was rather strange seeing its hallway and corridors so relatively quiet after the noise and bustle of the ball and none the less welcome for that.

A bespectacled young man, his hair a mass of black curls, hurried across the hallway carrying a small pile of papers. After a cursory check by yet another guard, he was allowed to pass through a pair of enormous doors into the room beyond.

"That is the ballroom, if you can remember from last night," said Bachini. "It is where the main part of the conference it taking place. Come, let us take a peek to see how things are getting along."

Once more Bachini negotiated our way past the guards and we slipped silently into the rear of the ballroom. It was an entirely different sight to the one I had seen the previous evening. No longer a sizeable open space populated by dancing couples in their ballgowns and evening suits, there was now a pair of big oak tables in the middle of the room, around which sat important looking men, each of whom wore a most serious demeanour. Dotted around the edge of the room was a series of other, smaller tables, at each of which sat a cluster of anxious-looking individuals whom I took to be the supporting officials for the diplomats at the big tables.

A general air of tension hung over the room, as if we might have arrived at some crucial moment, and I observed that the more senior diplomats were engaged in whispered conversations with one or more of their adjutants. We watched for a while, curious to see the conference in operation.

Bachini leaned in close to me. "Count Villafranca looks more serious than he did last night."

I nodded, not having immediately recognised Villafranca, who looked altogether a different man to the one I had seen so briefly at the ball. I looked around the central tables again, realising I had not noticed the most important delegate at the conference, the Sultan of Zanzire. No, I had not missed him, he was not there. Indeed there was a rather obvious gap in the ranks seated around the main tables.

"No sign of the Sultan," I whispered to Bachini.

She looked again at those sat around the central tables.

"Perhaps that is why the others are all in conversations of their own. Taking the opportunity to debate things while he is temporarily absent," she suggested.

At that moment, a splendidly-attired soldier appeared at Bachini's shoulder. He spoke briefly to her in Italian before she turned back to me and gestured that I needed to follow her.

We stepped out into the hallway to find Colonel Morelli waiting for us, accompanied by his now familiar adjutant, and there was something in the Colonel's grey-blue eyes that had me concerned even before he spoke.

"Bachini. Templeman," he said, his voice uncharacteristically quiet. "I have unfortunate news. It seems the Kaiser's men did have another plan, after all. The Sultan's son has been kidnapped and is being held to ransom."

DESPERATE NEWS

I was, for a moment, speechless. Had we really been so easily outwitted?

"But how?" asked Bachini.

"It was on the road here, some twenty-five or so minutes ago," replied Morelli, looking glum. "I imagine you would have passed through the same spot not so long ago yourselves. The motor vehicles were forced off the road and the escort overwhelmed."

"What have the Germans demanded for his release?" asked Bachini, seeming to bristle with frustration and anger.

"Officially it is not the Germans who have taken him," replied the Colonel. "The Sultan has received a letter from a group calling themselves the Freedom Fighters for Erteria and it is they who are claiming responsibility. They demand to be a self-governing region within the Sultanate and insist that the Germans be allowed to enter the enclave as a guarantor of the new arrangements."

"And any new government will be a puppet of the Germans. How convenient," snapped Bachini.

"Indeed," responded Morelli.

We had to pause our conversation as we waited for two officials of the French delegation to pass by. Once they were gone, I made my first contribution to the conversation.

"Does it seem likely the Sultan will acquiesce? I understand he has only the one son."

"I have just come from a meeting with the Sultan. Our Prime Minister has persuaded him to allow us forty-eight hours to find his son and return him safely to his father. If either the forty-eight hours should expire or anything untoward happen to the son, the Sultan will agree to the demands made on him. He was very reluctant to allow us any time at all to undertake a rescue," added Morelli.

"He must be under considerable pressure," I observed. "Aside from the personal aspect, should anything happen to the Sultan's heir it would be certain to foster unrest amongst the resulting claimants to the Sultanate. Civil war could even follow."

"And that too would present the Germans with an opportunity to intervene in Erteria," added Bachini.

"They would win in either event," said Morelli. "Unless we are successful in rescuing the son."

An unpleasant thought occurred to me. "You don't think it's possible the plan to assassinate Villafranca was nothing more than a smokescreen, do you? An attempt to take our eyes off the real target?"

The Colonel wrinkled his large nose. "I asked myself the same question and I believe it could be so. Once the assassin had been dealt with, it was inevitable that everyone relaxed a little, perhaps making it easier for the kidnapping. It seems to me it was too well-planned to have been made up at short notice."

"And we thought it was to be Von Luck and his friends who would be looking worried today," I said, with a little shake of the head.

"Do we have any idea where the Sultan's son has been taken? Any sightings or reports?" asked Bachini, clearly keen to make a start.

"Some villagers who heard gunfire after the escort was attacked reported seeing two motor vehicles racing along the road towards Rome, but we have no idea yet where they went after that. However," continued Morelli, in a rather more upbeat tone, "the police escort did not let the attackers have things all their own way. One of them was shot. He is dead, unfortunately, but we believe him to be a Georgian. Possibly in the employ of the notorious Gregor Lomidze."

I was startled at the mention of that name and Morelli noticed my look of shock.

"You know of Lomidze?" he asked.

"I do, indeed," I replied, as recollection of an especially unpleasant mission to Vienna came flooding back to me. "In fact, I had something of a run-in with the criminal in Vienna. I was most fortunate to escape with my life."

"He is reported to be highly resourceful and prepared to undertake practically any mission if the payment is great enough," responded the Colonel.

"He is certainly resourceful. If he is involved here then it is, without question, going to make our task all the more difficult. However, I would be immensely surprised to find him here, in Italy. He is a wanted man in many countries, not least of all by His Majesty's Government."

"Perhaps he has chosen to manage matters from afar," suggested Morelli. "He must surely have able deputies he can send to undertake the kidnapping itself."

"Either way," cut in Bachini. "It allows the German government to claim they have had no involvement in the kidnapping, which will suit them."

"I am afraid so, Bachini. But we must proceed with our rescue attempts, all the same. I have given orders that a special team be put together at once, of which I will personally take charge," said Morelli. "Our agents will work alongside the police to comb every inch of Rome and the surrounding countryside. Both of you will, of course, be part of that team. We will return to headquarters now and begin drawing up our plans."

"What about the conference?" asked Bachini, as we turned to make our way out to a waiting motor vehicle.

"It is to be delayed by forty-eight hours," replied Morelli. "An announcement will be made shortly. It is possible that, if our efforts at a rescue are unsuccessful, the conference will not be resumed. Matters might no longer be open to negotiation, should such a scenario arise."

DISASTER

Given the serious reversal in our fortunes, I persuaded the Colonel to drop me off at the British Embassy, assuring him I would make my own way to his headquarters. Whilst I knew the Ambassador was now at the Villa Carlota, I was hoping that Captain Hannah might have arrived back from his time with the Italian army. I was very keen on providing him with a personal update on the latest, unwelcome, developments. It was also my route to updating Sir Joshua, who would, otherwise, have to wait for news to reach him via standard diplomatic channels.

To my relief, I found that Hannah was, indeed, back at the embassy and free of other engagements.

"Only arrived back about five minutes ago," announced the Captain, as he closed the door to his private office. "Part of the day's exercises had to be postponed until tomorrow, though it wasn't entirely clear why, I must say."

"Well, I'm jolly glad for that," I said, taking a seat as Hannah sat down in his chair behind a small teak desk.

"You look a little harassed," commented Hannah as he glanced at several envelopes that lay on his in-tray. "Been doing too much sightseeing? It can get a little overwhelming after a while, what with there being so much history and culture to be found here."

"I wish that were so," I replied. "But I'm afraid things are rather more serious than that. The Sultan's only son has been kidnapped and a demand received that essentially hands the Kaiser everything he wants from the conference."

Hannah stared at me in silence for a moment.

"When did this happen?" he asked, leaning forward on to his desk.

"I've come straight from the Villa Carlota. Colonel Morelli was there and updated me and the Italian agent, Bachini, personally. It seems the kidnapping happened not long after we arrived at the Villa. There was an exchange of gunfire when the escort was forced off the road on its way to the villa, but the police were overwhelmed and the Sultan's son hasn't been seen since."

"My word. I bet the Italians are feeling bad about that," replied Hannah, with a look of astonishment. "Is a rescue attempt going to be made?"

"It is. The head of the Italian secret service, Colonel Morelli, will be taking charge personally and it sounds as if they will be putting every man they have into the effort."

I puffed out my cheeks. Things had turned around so quickly and I hated the idea of being bettered by Von Luck.

"There something more to it?" asked Hannah, with impressive perception.

"Oh, it seems there's someone involved that I had a run-in with in Vienna not long ago. A Georgian named Gregor Lomidze. I had rather hoped I wouldn't need to have anything to do with him ever again."

"I know that name," responded Hannah. "Gun-runner and the like, if I'm not mistaken. Colourful character, I hear."

"Colourful? Yes, I suppose he is," I replied.

The phone on Hannah's desk rang. He answered and gave instructions he wasn't to be disturbed until further notice.

"So, what can I do for you?" he asked, sitting back in his chair.

"The Ambassador is at the Villa now, so he'll get the official update soon enough, but I'd like to pass on a personal update as there will no doubt be things the Italian Government won't want to mention, for now at least. I'd also like the update passed on to Sir Joshua, back in London; otherwise, it will be some time before he hears anything."

"Of course," said Hannah. "What is it you want me to pass on?"

I provided him with a summary of everything I knew up to that point and the, as yet, unspecified plans to rescue the Sultan's only son.

"Things could get very difficult if the Sultan is forced to agree to such terms," observed the Captain, once I had finished speaking. "I don't imagine the other Great Powers will simply sit idly by and watch the Germans walk into Erteria."

"It's a wonder they think there is any possibility of that happening," I replied, glancing at the clock on the narrow mantelpiece above the small fireplace.

"I suspect you want to get on," said Hannah, having noticed my restlessness. "I only wish I could do more to help you. To be honest, I wouldn't mind getting involved in something altogether more exciting. My work here isn't all that demanding and I'm not really cut out to sit behind a desk for most of the day."

He got to his feet and we shook hands.

"It's funny you should say that," I said. "Sometimes I think I'm not altogether suited to all these nerve-shredding assignments I find myself on."

I smiled, as if in jest, but knew deep down there was an element of truth in my words.

"Well, if there is anything else I can do for you, don't hesitate to ask. And best of luck," added Hannah as I stepped out into the hallway.

Relieved to have found Hannah back from his excursion and my update left safely in his hands, I strode out of the embassy and called over a cab, my mind shifting focus to the not inconsiderable demands of the chase that now lay ahead. If we had enjoyed some good fortune in tracking down the Egyptian, then I suspected it would be more challenging to find the Sultan's son. It was a daunting prospect.

The driver held open the cab door for me and I climbed in, a dozen or more thoughts racing through my head at the same time. I suppose that was the reason I didn't notice, until I sat down, a man sitting in the seat opposite me. He held a revolver in one hand, pointed directly at me. I went to lunge for him, but the man behind pulled me back and I felt his own revolver as he jabbed it into my ribs before climbing in to join his colleague.

The first one, a taller man with a narrow, weathered face, tapped on the roof then smiled at me as the cab lurched forward.

"What do you want?" I demanded.

But the man just continued smiling and shook his head. It seemed another kidnapping was under way and I cursed myself for my lack of observation. I was hardly going to be able to do much to help the efforts at tracking down the Sultan's son if I was locked in some dark, damp cellar. Indeed, it was possible that resources might be diverted in order to find and rescue me. And what an even bigger fool I would feel then.

A PRISONER

The journey on which I was taken lasted some twenty minutes, as best I could judge. With the blinds pulled down I could see nothing of the outside world and, though I tried hard to do so, it was difficult to make out much from the sounds that passed over and around us, especially given the clatter from the cab wheels and the horse's hooves.

At one point we stopped momentarily and I heard a woman's voice call out, shrill and demanding, as clearly as if she had been standing directly in front of me. But, alas, she spoke in Italian and I could understand not a word of what she said.

For a while I allowed myself to wallow and fester in self-pity and frustration but, with a concerted effort, I dragged myself out of that place and determined to make what I could of the situation. I began with a study of my two captors and realised, with some little surprise, that neither of them looked the least bit like Georgians. I was familiar with the profile of a typical Georgian after my still recent run-in with Gregor Lomidze and his private army in Vienna. They had, almost to a man, been thick-set, swarthy types, partial to a generous beard and careless of their attire. They were also invariably coarse in their behaviour, unlike Lomidze himself, who, it seemed, had acquired more refined manners during his years of travel.

The men guarding me did not fit this profile at all. They were not at all thick set and, although simply attired, their clothes were of a better cut and made from superior materials. They also appeared to take more care of their personal hygiene and both had recently shaved. My suspicion was they were Italians, not Georgians.

I decided to put my hypothesis to the test in the simplest way possible.

"Who are you and where are you taking me?" I demanded.

Both simply stared back at me, silent and unmoving.

I tried again, this time leaning forward and directing myself at the taller man. "You there, where are you taking me? I am a British citizen and I demand to know what's going on here?"

My sudden movement did the trick. The shorter man jabbed his revolver forward, pressing it against my chest, and snapped back at me with the single word, "No."

It was only one word, but it was enough for me to hear his Italian accent. So, they were local men, hired, I had to assume, by Von Luck and his cronies. Perhaps the Georgians were fully occupied with the Sultan's son and Von Luck had been obliged to fall back on local criminals in order to avoid the direct involvement of his own men.

It occurred to me that such men, bought for money, might succumb to a superior counter-offer.

"Whatever Von Luck is paying you, the British Government will double," I proposed, pronouncing my words with care.

Of course, I could not know whether or not either man spoke English but, if they did, they chose not to show it, for both remained silent, their features showing no sign of emotion, their guns still pointed at me.

I sat back, folded my arms across my chest and closed my eyes. Perhaps I would still not be able to make out anything useful from the sounds I heard outside as we clattered along, but I might as well make the effort, as there was clearly little else to be done.

*

In matter of fact, we had continued on our way for barely another five minutes when the carriage began to slow and then stopped. I heard a brief exchange between two deep male voices from outside, close by the carriage door, both speaking in Italian. This was followed by the sound of running feet.

I opened my eyes as the taller of my captors opened the carriage door and climbed out. Light flooded into the gloom, briefly dazzling me. My eyes had still not fully adjusted when I felt the shorter man's revolver jab painfully into my ribs and a hand push me towards the doorway. I complied and stepped out into a small, enclosed courtyard, its cobbled surface surrounded on all sides by tall stone buildings that were somewhat rundown. The smell of dilapidation, damp and festering, filled my nostrils.

I was pushed towards an open doorway, flanked on either side by tall, stern-faced men armed with revolvers. I was led down an unlit hallway and my eyes now struggled to adapt once more to the gloom, causing me to bump my head painfully on the low-set frame of a doorway when we passed into a high-ceilinged, small and rectangular space. To our left was a set of narrow wooden stairs that were in such a bad state of repair they looked as if they might not bear the weight of a man. I was directed to make my way up them.

By this point I had reached one rather welcome conclusion. My captors were hardly likely to have gone to so much trouble if all they intended to do was kill me. A bullet in the back of the head in the small courtyard would have been all that was required, had that been their intention.

For a moment I nearly smiled at this thought as, upon

reaching the top of the stairs, I was nudged along a narrow landing. But I thought better of it, in case it should elicit a violent response.

However, my relief was rather short-lived. Clearly there was some sort of plan at work here and the options that sprang to mind were not welcome ones. My earlier notion that it might be an attempt to divert resources away from the hunt for the Sultan's son seemed vaguely plausible, though surely of little consequence given the extent of the manpower available.

I did briefly consider that an attempt might be made to use me as some sort of bargaining chip, but Sir Joshua would be a fool to allow such a thing to happen and a fool he most certainly was not. Capture and potential death were risks that we signed up to when we joined the service. We all knew that, however much we tried to turn a blind eye to such possibilities.

The more worrying prospect was that my captors intended to interrogate me. Refusing to answer their questions was easy enough, but the threat of torture was another matter entirely and a fear swept over me that I might not be strong enough to avoid giving away information that was detrimental to my colleagues. I would rather die than expose them to any possibility of danger. It was an unsettling notion, but one for which I began to steel myself.

We passed two doors, both on our right, before reaching a third at the end of the hallway. It's frame and lock had clearly been recently replaced, in complete contrast to the others, which looked as if they might fall down in the merest gust of a breeze. The door was opened and, with another jab of a revolver in my now bruised ribs, I was obliged to step into the room. Before I even had time to turn around I heard the door slam shut and the key turn in the lock.

Was I, perhaps, to be left to fester and worry before they began their interrogation? It was another unpleasant and unwelcome thought, which I brushed away at once before turning back to face the room and begin assessing my chances of escape.

My prison cell was six paces from side-to-side and five from the door to the outer wall. Two large windows, devoid of their glass, had been well boarded over, the timbers yielding nothing when I tested them. The only light that came into the room did so via the uneven gaps between these boards, particles of dust dancing in these narrow shafts of sunlight that fell upon the naked floorboards in an erratic pattern of lines.

The walls and ceiling had once been covered in plaster but now great lumps were missing, their remnants scattered in decaying piles across the floor and the stench of dry rot was unmistakable. A scurrying in one corner told me I was sharing the room with a rodent cellmate.

A thorough search of my new accommodation found no means of a way out other than via the door through which I had entered. It was not a promising situation and I was wondering what schemes I could come up with in order to overcome my guards when I heard the key turn in the lock. I looked across the room to see the door swing open and two unsettlingly large men walk in ahead of a short, round man who wheezed in a manner that spoke of ill health.

"Mister Templeman," began the round man in heavily-accented English. "I have heard much about you and Miss Bachini in the last few days. It is my pleasure to meet such a respected Englishman, though it is unfortunate we could not meet under more friendly circumstances."

Another man appeared, carrying a solidly built wooden chair, which he placed in the middle of the room.

"Please, Mr Templeman," said the round man, gesturing to the chair. "Take a seat." I hesitated. "I must insist, or else Luca and Mattia will help you sit down." He spoke in a manner that bordered on friendly, but his face remained impassive.

I stepped across the room and sat down, steeling myself for the violence I was sure was to follow, sending up prayers that I would turn out to have the strength and determination needed not to give anything away.

INTERROGATION

The round man sat down in front of me on his own chair and, for a moment, studied me as if he might be searching for weaknesses in my defences. My breathing had become a little shallow and my heart rate had increased, though I doubted he would be able to detect such things and I concentrated on meeting his searching gaze.

"My employers are very keen that you are kept off the streets of our fine city for a day or two," stated my gaoler. "That, as you see, has been easy enough to arrange. But they are also curious. Curious to know how your friends in the Italian secret service intend to look for the Sultan's son. He is not a strong young man, I am told," the round man added, with more than a little contempt in his voice. "My associates inform me that he cries like a child and makes promises of much money in return for his freedom. Such a disappointment."

"Kidnapping is not a pleasant experience," I pointed out.

"So I hear," replied the round man, the air drawing in and out of his lungs in a shallow, uncomfortable manner. "Though I have never enjoyed the experience myself. I take good care to ensure such an… unfortunate situation does not arise."

"You should try it some time. I heartily recommend it," I replied, attempting to appear indifferent to my predicament.

He wheezed some more, then took an ugly green and blue handkerchief from a pocket and began to dab at the sweat forming on his large forehead. I could see now that the plain white shirt he wore was a little too small, the material stretched across his sizeable stomach, and his heavy brown shoes were in need of a polish.

Everything seemed an effort for him, his movements a little slow, laboured even, as if he resented expending the energy. I found I did not much like him, but, then again, that was no great surprise, not given the circumstances in which I found myself.

"Now then," he began, as he folded his handkerchief and pushed it back into his pocket. "Tell me, where do Morelli and his men intend to begin their search? Here, in Rome, perhaps?"

I held back from giving any answer at first, not that I had the least idea where Morelli would be beginning his search. Why make things any easier for my captors than they needed to be? When I did speak, I spoke the truth, not having sufficient knowledge of the city and its surrounding countryside to be able to make an attempt at sending my enemies on a wild goose chase.

"I have not the least idea. If you recall, your men grabbed me from outside the British Embassy and that was before I had a chance to join Morelli and Bachini at their headquarters."

"But you travelled back to Rome with them from the Villa Carlotta. You cannot ask me to believe that you did not discuss the matter then, even in more general terms."

I took my time once more, casting an eye over the men standing guard over me, before answering.

"We had no information on which to base any such decisions. It was the Colonel's intention to assess the situation once he was back in Rome, then to allocate his resources. He is, after all, a military man and someone like that prefers to be in possession of whatever intelligence is available before they deploy their forces."

I could feel sweat beginning to form in my armpits, despite the coolness of the room.

"You make it sound like a military operation. Is that the plan, to make use of the army as well as the police?"

"Again, I've no idea, though if I were Morelli I would deploy all the men I could get hold of, the army included. Wouldn't you do the same?" I challenged.

The round man watched me closely. His small grey eyes were unsettling, despite their washy nature, and it took some forceful effort on my part not to look away, which I knew would be seen as a sign of weakness.

He was about to speak again when the door swung open and in stepped a young fellow; an urchin, of sorts, looking like something straight out of a Dickens novel. He handed a folded piece of paper to the round man, who looked a little disgruntled at the interruption as he snatched it up. Unfolding it, my interrogator made an exaggerated matter of reading the note, holding it at arm's length. Long-sighted, I concluded, and without the benefit of his glasses.

Having satisfied himself he had gleaned whatever he needed to from the message, the round man folded the piece of paper back in two with surprising care before slipping it into a jacket pocket.

"I am afraid I am called away on urgent business," he announced, directing his remark at me with more than a hint of disappointment in his voice. "Such a shame. We will have to continue our conversation a little later, though I hope not to keep you waiting long."

"I imagine you will still find me here when you return. It is not as if I have other plans," I replied, as sarcastically as I could manage.

He ignored my comment and dismissed the lad with a cursory wave of the hand.

"A drink would be much appreciated," I ventured, thinking I ought to make such a request while I had the chance to do so.

"Of course," answered my host, before saying something to one of his henchmen. "Luca will bring you some water. Now, do make yourself comfortable. You may be wise to sleep for a while, as we are likely to be busy when I return. We have much information to extract from you," he added, before breaking into an extended, bronchial cough that caused his face to turn a sickly shade of red.

I felt, all of a sudden, rather distressed. A day that had started out so well was seemingly to end, for me at least, very badly indeed.

A BID FOR FREEDOM

My gaolers left the room and once more I heard the key turn in the lock, followed by the sound of footsteps retreating quickly along the corridor. Then all was silent, save for the regular beating of my heart and the passage of air to and from my lungs, both of which seemed to have become so much more pronounced.

It was impossible not to wonder what it was that had caused the round man to depart so suddenly when my interrogation seemed a matter of some importance. Could it, I hoped, be news that Morelli had already found and rescued the Sultan's son? What joy that would bring me. It did, though, occur to me that if that was indeed the news then the opportunity to take revenge on me might prove too much to resist. That, however, was not a prospect that much changed my predicament.

I pulled my watch from my jacket pocket and found that some forty minutes had passed since I had been abducted from outside the embassy and that it was now two-fifteen. I kicked my heel against the wall, then began to pace the room in slow, repetitive circles, thinking that I must be able to come up with some plan of escape, even if it might be a little desperate.

Some ten minutes later, Luca returned with a glass of water, which he placed on the dusty floor only after I had retreated to the far side of the room. A wise course of action, since I would otherwise have taken the opportunity to launch myself at him. I picked up the glass, took it across the room and sat down against the outside wall in a deep funk.

At some point, I fell into a doze and awoke with a start as I felt myself falling away to one side. I shook my head, yawned then stretched my arms. My watch told me I had been asleep for no more than twenty minutes. As I slipped it back into my pocket, I heard again the sound of scurrying and, looking to my left, saw a small brown mouse poking about in the broken plaster in the corner of the room. It stopped, sniffed the air in a most determined fashion, then turned around and made its way, in fits and starts, to a broken section of wall, through which it passed from my sight.

I scratched my chin as a moment's hope settled upon me. Getting to my feet I walked over to where the mouse had vanished and, squatting down by the wall, began to push and poke at the plaster and timber. I found that the timbers in the wall were not, as I would have expected them to be, solid lengths of good quality wood, but thin pliable strips that had been woven to form a flexible board of sorts, on to which the plaster had been laid.

Sections of this feeble material were already heavily decayed and it took very little effort from me to remove yet more until I had opened up a gap large enough for a middling size dog to pass through. Excitement began to well up inside me. It seemed I owed that little mouse my considerable thanks. But how to make the opening larger still? I looked over at the glass and a thought occurred to me.

I had not heard Luca retreat down the hallway after he had brought me my water. so had to assume he was outside, standing guard. That might be a problem for what I had in mind. Pressing my ear against the door, I listened for signs of life and was rewarded by hearing a clear, rhythmic snoring. It was impossible not to smile.

Picking up the glass, I dropped it on to a length of timber from which protruded a fat, rusty nail. The glass broke on impact, offering me three large, sharp-edged sections. I reached down and collected one up.

As I hoped, the sharp edge on the glass cut through the wooden slivers sufficiently for me to then be able to break them apart. After ten minutes' work, taking great care to make as little noise as possible, I had opened a rough-edged hole through which I was able to squeeze into the room beyond with only a small amount of difficulty.

I found myself in another abandoned, dusty room, although this one was in an even more dilapidated state than the one I had just left; whole sections of plaster had fallen from the walls and the ceiling. The door had come away from its hinges and sat, covered in dust, propped against the wall.

However, a window at the end of the room still retained its glass and was not boarded over. I stepped gingerly over and around the piles of plaster and sections of broken timber, ever aware of the possibility of a broken floorboard, and rubbed away an area of dust from the window, so I could take a look outside.

To my left was the courtyard where I had been bundled out of the carriage. In front of me was the roof of a single-storey room and beyond that a brick-walled alleyway that ran away from the building I was in and on past several others. I felt a burst of excitement as I looked down upon my route to freedom.

I took hold of the lock on the window and began to test it. It was rusty and it took some little effort to free it enough so that I could begin to lift it. A shrill note rang out, setting my teeth on edge, and I immediately froze, directing all my efforts to listening for sounds of movement in the hallway.

There were none, but as I steeled myself to set about the lock again I heard a man's voice call from below. He called a second time, sounding disgruntled. When still there was no response I heard footsteps, heavy on the stairs. I had no certainty that the window would open if I gave it my all but knew I would be discovered should it make much noise, so I stepped cautiously across the room, pressing myself up against the inner wall where the plaster looked to be still solidly attached.

The footsteps reached the top of the stairs and this time when the same voice called out it brought back a response from Luca. There was an exchange between the two men as I glanced back at the window, but all that did was to ratchet up the anxiety I was feeling. Freedom was so close at hand I could almost taste it.

One of the men strode quickly along the hallway and descended the stairs at pace. After a moment's silence, that felt like an eternity, I heard the other walking more slowly along the corridor. Though I could not see him, I could feel the man's presence, as he stood by the broken doorway. There came the sound of a match being struck before a long, thin arm of cigarette smoke reached into the room.

My heart was racing now and my breathing had become shallow and rapid. I formed my hands into tight fists and set myself ready to launch forward and to fight.

There was a shuffling of feet that brought me to the very point of throwing myself towards the doorway, then the sound of footsteps along the hallway and the creak of wood as if the man had just sat down on a chair.

I wasted no more time and returned to the window. There was to be no more tentative teasing and testing of the lock. I forced it abruptly across before taking the frame in both hands and heaving upwards. There came a loud, piercing squeal as timber that had not been moved in years was dragged forcibly apart, then the welcome sensation of a cool breeze across my face,

But almost at once there came a loud, guttural shout from the hallway and the sound of a chair falling to the floor. There was no time to climb out on to the roof below and scramble across it to safety without real risk of taking a bullet in the back. My brain raced for another option and I flew across the room to press myself hard up against the wall by the doorway.

He swept into the room with quick sharp strides, a short,

bulky man with large hands, in one of which he wielded a revolver, and raced across to the open window. I wasted not a moment. Snatching up a length of timber, I advanced towards him.

He half-turned on hearing my footsteps but was too late. I struck as violent a blow as I could manage, right against the back of his head. He staggered, his weapon slipping from his grasp and clattering to the floor, before a simple trip from my outstretched leg was all that was required to leave him in a crumpled, groaning heap.

There was another shout from the bottom of the stairs, but I ignored that, grabbed the revolver then climbed out through the open window. It was fortunate that I did not immediately set off across the shallow-angled roof for, had I done so, I would almost certainly have tumbled from it. Everywhere there were missing or broken tiles and short exposed sections of the roof beams. I hesitated, not certain how best to navigate it.

That almost cost me my life. From the small, open courtyard came more angry shouts followed at once by the report of a gun and two little explosions of shards from the stone wall beside me. I dropped down low and half slid, half stumbled across the roof, as the air around me filled with the sound of breaking tiles and more gunshots.

I slipped without control over the edge of the roof and fell to the cobbled ground below in a reckless heap. That fall left my right shoulder and hip burning with pain as I clambered uncertainly to my feet, momentarily confused as to my bearings.

More sharp reports from a gun and this time bullets zipped off the stone wall behind me. I glanced up, saw Luca leaning out of the window I had clambered through and fired off three shots of my own. As he ducked back inside I turned and raced for all I was worth along the narrow alleyway, ignoring the pain and the struggle for breath. Ahead lay freedom.

AN OPPORTUNITY

The alleyway opened up on to a short street populated with a mix of stone-built residences and business premises. It was another poor looking place, one where the few people I could see were too intent on scraping together a living to pay much heed to a stranger such as I.

Short of breath and my hip and shoulder stinging, I stopped and leaned back against a wall, my breathing heavy and my shirt sticky against my back. As yet there was no sign of pursuit and I could only guess the alleyway gate that led through to the courtyard must have been locked, forcing my gaolers to find some other way over or round the enclosing wall.

A small child, a girl I believe, appeared and stood watching me, a tiny, battered wooden horse held loosely in one hand. I attempted a smile, but fear it was more a grimace. Either way, her response was to run off without a word, swinging the wooden horse by her side.

As my breathing began to settle and the thumping of my heart slowed, I stepped forward towards the near end of the street, which I could see let out on to a much wider and more populous avenue. My wits were sufficiently recovered that I made a mental note of the largest of the business premises I could see. It was possible the round man and his associates might be taken if the police could fall upon them in short order.

I was in luck. As I stepped out into the wider avenue, I

almost at once saw a police officer ambling along the road. I think at first he might have preferred to avoid the dishevelled and bruised figure that lurched towards him, almost certain to be a drunken waster, but as soon I spoke Morelli's name the man's attitude changed entirely and he could hardly have been more helpful, although he understood little of what I was saying.

Ten minutes later, I was drinking a welcome cup of coffee in a police station while a phone call was being put through to the headquarters of the Italian secret service.

*

It was Bachini who came to take me back to her headquarters. She was relieved in the extreme. My disappearance had not gone unnoticed and frantic efforts had been made to track me down, with all concerned well aware of what had happened to Stoneman. Their efforts had been undermined by several false sightings which they suspected had been put about in a deliberate effort to throw the police off the scent. It also came as something of a surprise to Bachini when I mentioned that the men who had snatched me from outside the embassy were Italians, not Georgians nor yet Germans. Bringing in yet another party was not without its risks and it suggested our adversaries had not the manpower themselves to undertake such an action.

Morelli was equally pleased to see me and arranged for me to receive medical attention. He also pointed out that it was most fortunate I had escaped, for he could not see how the round man would have been able to let me live once he had shown himself to me. As it was, when I described the round man, Morelli knew at once who he was; a criminal of some stature and reputation.

As for the Sultan's son, Morelli reported there had been no progress in finding him, despite several hundred police and soldiers having been assigned to the task. A carefully-laid plan had been drawn up and every square foot of the city would be searched, though whether this could be completed within the time available seemed highly unlikely. Police in the villages that dotted the countryside within a ten-mile radius of Rome had also been told to be vigilant.

But Morelli was keen we should not let slip the opportunity to sweep up the round man and his accomplices. The location of the building was soon enough established, once they had my description of it and the name of the business premises I had noted, and a small, well-armed force of police and Morelli's own men was promptly assembled. I insisted on joining them and our little convoy of motor-vehicles set off barely an hour after Bachini and I had arrived back at her headquarters.

AN EXPLOSIVE ENCOUNTER

There was not a cloud in the sky and a warm sun had shone down on us as we drove across the city to a hoped for meeting with the round man. Now, however, as Bachini and I hid low in the shadows of an empty tenement, the air was cool to the point of almost being cold and I pulled my jacket more closely about me.

In front of us and on the other side of the street armed police officers crouched, poised for action, their faces hidden in the shadows. Beyond them, closing in on a large wooden gate that led to a courtyard, were two other men, carrying a small explosive charge that would be used to blow the gates.

"Morelli is definitely sure they are still in there?" I asked Bachini again.

She smiled, as a parent would towards a small, uncertain child.

"He is. Don't worry, Alex, we will get them. And, hopefully, they will sing us a tune once they realise it's in their own interests."

I didn't have any reason to doubt Morelli. My restlessness was really the result of an anxiety that came from such a deep-seated desire to capture the round man. He could very well turn out to be our best means of locating the Sultan's son.

"They're nearly there," whispered Bachini as the two explosives men approached the gates.

We both of us shuffled a little as we readied ourselves.

Once the gates were blown, our advance guard would rush in, followed by the rest of us. The alleyway that had been my route to freedom was heavily guarded, as were the two streets either side of the little complex of tumbledown buildings and open courtyard. There was no possible way out for anyone in that building.

"They've stopped," I said, my voice low, as the two advancing men paused.

"They must have heard something," suggested Bachini.

The two men signalled each other then quickly retreated to their starting positions at either end of the courtyard wall. They had barely done so when there came the sound of motor-vehicles, their engines revving high as the gates to the yard were flung open. Startled, both Bachini and I instinctively fell back against the wall.

At once gunfire exploded from all directions as two vehicles swept out of the courtyard and surged forward, on to the road. All was noise and violence, a cacophony of rifle and revolver reports and screaming vehicle engines assaulting my head and making it almost impossible to think clearly. Bachini, however, had already raised her gun and fired off her first shots at the lead vehicle. I, a little slower to react, then brought up my own weapon and began to fire.

As I did so, I saw him, sitting in the front passenger seat of the lead vehicle, firing out of the open window with a look on his face of raw, unadulterated excitement. It was Von Luck and there, seated behind him, flanked by two other men, was the figure of a younger man, his skin dark, his features drawn and frightened.

"The Sultan's son," I shouted over the din.

"What?" came the confused reply.

"The Sultan's son," I repeated, no longer firing my revolver. "In the back of the first vehicle."

Bachini lowered her own weapon, though by now it made little difference. The two vehicles roared along the street, sending up great clouds of choking dust, and were beyond our reach in mere moments.

We both got to our feet and stared in silence at the dust cloud, briefly unaware of the pandemonium all around us. I didn't need to ask Bachini what she was thinking because it would be the same as I was. We had all but taken the Sultan's son in our grasp, even if unexpectedly, and now he was gone, swept away from us so frustratingly.

I was soon enough snapped out of my thoughts by the continued shouting and rushing all around us. From a side street came the roar of a vehicle engine as it was started up. On the far side of the road, I could see Morelli directing a group of men towards the courtyard, while another hurried in the direction of our parked vehicles.

"We need to get in one of the vehicles being sent after Von Luck," I insisted, looking round at Bachini.

She was about to answer when there was an enormous flash from the direction of the courtyard and the whole world was ripped asunder by a violent, ear-splitting explosion. I felt the ground quite literally shake beneath my feet and briefly caught sight of bricks and stonework hurtling in all directions before a violent blast of hot air knocked from me from my feet, throwing me away like a toy doll. I was slammed against a wall, momentarily held there, then fell towards the ground, already unconscious.

THE PATIENT

A light, round and bleary, stared down at me as I began to open my eyes. At first, the glare was too much and my eyes struggled to adjust. I was on my back, looking up at a ceiling. My mouth was dry and I was increasingly aware of aches and pains practically all over my body. I tried to speak, but something more like a croak came out.

I took a deep breath and, as I did so, I felt the touch of crisp, clean cotton sheets against my skin. Turning my head a little to one side, I could see I was in a small hospital ward of sorts, with three other beds occupied by injured parties like me.

A voice spoke from the other side and I looked back to see a nurse standing there, smiling. She reached down with a thermometer and eased it between my crusty lips. After a moment she took it back, read it, nodded her head approvingly then wrote something on a set of notes.

"Ah, you're awake." The voice was a familiar one.

I tilted my head fully to the side and there, beyond the nurse, was Morelli. He was wiping his face with a towel, his clothes covered in a thick layer of dust and debris. I could see the backs of his hands were scarred with a multitude of small cuts and bruises and I recalled how close he had been to the courtyard when the explosion happened. It was miraculous he had managed to survive.

The nurse helped me to sit up, then handed me a glass of water and two small white tablets. I swallowed the tablets, along with most of the water.

"Thank Heavens, you're still alive," I said to Morelli, before coughing loudly.

"It seems my good deeds have paid back handsomely," he responded, handing the now dirty towel to the nurse, who said something to him in Italian.

As she left the room, Morelli pulled up a chair and sat down next to me, dust falling from his clothes on to the spotlessly clean floor.

"She says you are fine now. Just some cuts and bruises."

"Bachini?" I asked, worried for my friend.

"She is no worse than you and, like you, will be back on her feet soon enough."

I was pleased to hear that. But then another thought came to me; one that did not leave me feeling so happy."

"Von Luck. Was he in that building with me all the time?"

"It would seem so. We had no reports of vehicles arriving there after your escape. It was perhaps some staging post on the way to a more isolated location."

Morelli looked around the room, at the three other beds and I did likewise. The three occupants all appeared to be sleeping, one with a thick bandage wrapped around his head and an ugly cut on the side of his face.

"Not everyone was so fortunate," said Morelli, quietly.

There was a tiredness in the Colonel's voice that betrayed the unsurprising stress he was experiencing and his deep concern for his men. I set aside any further thoughts of Von Luck.

"Were many killed?" I asked, albeit reluctantly.

There was a pause before Morelli replied, in a quiet and sombre tone. "There are five dead and a dozen seriously injured. Many more with lesser injuries, though some of those will be unable to return to duty for the time-being. It is hard to know where they got so much explosive," he added, as if the thought had just that moment occurred to him.

I decided it was best to move the conversation on. "Is this a hospital?" I asked.

Morelli took a deep breath then shook his head. "No, this is our own medical facility. A recent addition for those like yourself with lesser injuries. The more serious cases still go to the city's public hospital, where there are the experts they need. This is the most use it has been put to since it opened."

The nurse reappeared, with two cups of coffee. She checked my temperature again and, satisfied I had not taken a sudden downturn, updated my medical notes once more, then left. I sipped my coffee and savoured the strong, aromatic taste with relish. It was, as they say, just what the doctor, or, in this case, the nurse ordered.

"There is much damage at the site of the explosion," continued Morelli. "The building you were captive in is all but destroyed and many of the surrounding buildings have suffered a good deal as well. I suspect it was a deliberate attempt to put my team out of action, not just a means of destroying any evidence we might have been able to find there."

"Surely you will take this up with the German government," I insisted. "Such a brazen attack on your men and right here in the centre of the city."

"I am sure our government will make strongly-worded representations to the Germans. But, if I was them, my response would simply be that Von Luck is no longer in their employ and is now acting on his own part, in some misguided act of patriotism. They will, no doubt, offer their sympathies and perhaps suggest they pay reparations as a gesture of goodwill. They might even offer to help track down Von Luck. Politicians are good at talking their way out of a tight corner, would you not agree?"

It was a cynical reply and Morelli almost sighed as he spoke the words, but it was difficult to object to the sentiment. "Sadly, yes, it is a skill they possess in abundance," I answered, wishing things were not so.

"But there are other ways to make these people pay," said Morelli in a rather cold tone, his head turned towards one of the small windows.

I thought it best not to enquire what such means might entail. Sometimes it is best not to know these things. I was about to take another drink of my coffee when I realised with a start there was one most important topic I had not yet asked the Colonel about.

"The Sultan's son, has anything been seen of him since he was driven off?" I asked.

Morelli shook his head. "Only two of our vehicles were able to take up the chase, due to the chaos of the explosion, and they were thrown off the scent very quickly. The last we saw of them they were heading east, but they must have veered off in another direction because we have been unable to find anything of them in that part of Rome."

"Surely they can't have gone far?" I insisted, almost in desperation.

"We have as many roads watched as we can manage, but it is impossible to cover them all," replied the Colonel. "It is possible they changed to other vehicles and have, perhaps, left the city. That's what I would have done if I was them. It is too risky to remain in Rome, especially after setting off that explosion. Every citizen who sees something or someone they believe to be suspicious will be sure to report it at once."

"Perhaps we will be lucky and they will be seen," I suggested, stifling a yawn.

It may have been the depressing thought of Von Luck escaping into the hills beyond Rome or, perhaps, to a waiting boat at some isolated fishing harbour, but I felt suddenly very tired. My head settled back against the pillow and my eyes closed. When I opened them again, Morelli was on his feet.

"You must rest, my friend. You will be of no use to me until you have done so. When we have news I will be sure to let you and Bachini know. Now, sleep, or else I will be in much trouble with the nurse."

I wanted to object to the suggestion that I needed sleep, but that felt like it was too much effort. I yawned, surprised I felt so tired so suddenly, my eyes beginning to close again.

The tablets the nurse had given me. Of course. My eyes flickered as I tried to open them, then closed and, with that, I fell into a deep sleep.

A SIGHTING IS REPORTED

I was sitting in a small office with Bachini and two other members of the Italian secret service. It was the following morning, a little after seven-thirty, and we were monitoring reports coming in from those searching for the Sultan's son. There were now over two thousand men swarming all over the city and surrounding hills but, as yet, there had been no sightings whatsoever of Von Luck and his men since they had blasted their way out of the courtyard the day before.

Bachini didn't say so, but I could detect in her mood that she was not altogether optimistic of our success. She had been quieter than was her normal way and her movements were sluggish, as if she felt disinclined to make the effort when there seemed so little prospect of reward.

We had less than twenty-four hours remaining in which to find the Sultan's son and the tension we were all feeling was palpable. I felt so useless, sitting there sifting through reports with Bachini. It didn't help that I couldn't read a word of what was written down, it all being in Italian, and had to rely on my colleague to translate and summarise for me.

At least, after a long, deep sleep during the night, something my body had clearly needed after the events of the previous afternoon, I now felt refreshed and alert. If only some news would come in that would allow me to put all the resulting energy to work.

I say there had been no sightings of Von Luck and that is

true, however it does not mean that there were no sightings reported. Several were, but all had turned out to be erroneous. A Dutch doctor, driving his son to visit an ailing aunt in Vignanello to the north of the capital, was stopped on a quiet country road by soldiers and held at gunpoint while police were called in to see whether or not they were Von Luck and the Sultan's son.

On another occasion, a group of fishermen in the coastal village of Ladispoli were confronted by a group of armed soldiers who had convinced themselves these men were the Germans trying to bundle the hostage on to a fishing boat and ferry him away elsewhere. Quite a sound idea, I thought, but, sadly, incorrect.

"This is devilishly frustrating," I finally admitted, slumping back in my chair.

Bachini put down the latest reports she had been looking through and rubbed at her nose.

"Yes, it is," she sighed. "I wish Colonel Morelli would change his mind and let us get out there. At least if we were doing something, something more than reading these reports, I'd feel like we were being useful."

A phone rang, sounding almost deafening in the near silence. We both turned our heads. One of the men working with us, Bruno, answered the call, listened briefly, spoke a few words in return, then put down the receiver. He looked across and shook his head before returning to the papers he was reading through.

I scratched the back of my neck, got to my feet and went and stood at the window, looking down on the narrow street below. It was empty, save for the same tatty old grey cat that had been sitting in a sunny doorway when I had looked out the window twenty minutes earlier. The emptiness of the street felt like a fitting metaphor for the emptiness of the reports we were receiving.

As I turned and began to walk back to my desk, the door swung open with a start and Morelli strode into the room. He clutched a sheet of paper in one hand and there was an alertness about his features that grabbed my attention at once. Something had happened.

"This is what we have been waiting for," he announced, holding up the sheet of paper, an animated look on his face. "It was brought straight to me just now. Two farm workers noticed that an abandoned farm outside the village of Bivio San Polo had been occupied, so they went closer to take a look. Fortunately for us they were cautious and, having satisfied themselves there were indeed people using the farmhouse they crept off home to tell their friends and family and to enquire if anyone knew anything about it. When the police arrived in the village a little later, they naturally got suspicious and took a look for themselves. It is Von Luck and his friends alright and we are moving in forces to surround them right now."

"What marvellous news," I bellowed, all my frustrations bursting out of me. "But where is Bivio San Polo?"

Morelli sought a map from one of the other men and spread it out on a desk.

"Here, in the hills to the east, beyond Tivoli" he said, pointing at a small rectangle at a crossroads. "The farm is just this side of the southern road. Apparently it sits in a little hollow, shielded from the road, which is no doubt why it was chosen."

"Do we know how many men Von Luck has there?" asked Bachini, leaning in to take a closer look at the map.

"The police report there are at least a dozen and it appears they have been there for some days."

"So, this was all planned," I suggested. "Not a spur of the moment affair."

"Indeed. Which means we must move with care. They will likely be ready for an attempt at a rescue and, if they become desperate enough, it is possible they might shoot the Sultan's son," replied Morelli.

It was an alarming thought, but one I had already considered. My ruthless Georgian friends were not ones to hold back from such an action, should they decide there was no longer anything to be gained from keeping a hostage alive. And Von Luck had already shown through his actions how cold and calculating he was capable of being.

"Are we to join the operation at Bivio San Polo?" asked Bachini, a look of expectation on her face.

"We are," answered Morelli, as he folded over the map. "We and another half dozen personnel from here are to make the journey there at once. I have given strict instructions that nothing is to be done until I am there. Not, that is, unless it is clear the Georgians are about to vacate the farm."

Bachini was reaching for her jacket even before the Colonel had finished speaking. The downcast mood of earlier was gone entirely, replaced by the energy and optimism I had come to know her for.

We departed for Bivio San Polo in two motor-vehicles less than five minutes later. With a little good fortune, another hour or so would see us shaking the Sultan's son warmly by the hand as we welcomed him back to freedom.

THE FARM

Tivoli was a beautiful little town with some fine buildings that may, on another occasion, have been most worthy of closer inspection. However, we passed through it at such a speed I hardly had an opportunity to take any of this in. Leaving its northern reaches, we found ourselves on a narrow, winding road, the air heavy with dust, no doubt thrown up by the unusually large volume of traffic that had so recently preceded us.

The land climbed steeply to our left and the hillside along its flanks was covered with thick woodland. To our right was open farmland, dotted here and there with small copses of trees. It was an idyllic scene, but one for which I had precious little time or interest, my mind focused now entirely on what lay ahead. I must admit, I was growing increasingly excited at the prospect of a final showdown with Von Luck and his Georgian associates, confident that our vastly superior numbers left no way for them to escape this time.

The vehicle groaned and rattled as we bumped and bounced along the roadway, slowing only a little as we entered the tiny village of Bivio San Polo. As we passed through, I observed there were small groups of bystanders at the roadside, no doubt curious as to why their little part of the world had suddenly attracted so much attention. If only they knew why we were there, they might have chosen to move to higher ground, from which they could watch the coming spectacle unfold.

Presently, as we skirted some woodland to the east, we came to a crossroads, beyond which the road narrowed yet further, to little more than a drover's track. Without any hesitation, our driver flung the vehicle into a right-hand turning, bringing us on to a stony, earthen track. We began to bounce and buck to such an extent that, finally, the driver was forced to slow down, though from the nature of his muttering he was unimpressed at this necessity.

Some four hundred yards further on a uniformed police officer stood sentinel in the road. As we approached, he raised an arm, directing us to turn into a small patch of scrub land where we parked our vehicles alongside others already there, hidden from prying eyes by a rocky outcrop on one side and woodland on the other. As I climbed out of our vehicle, my back and neck aching, I felt cool mountain air touch my skin and fill my lungs and was surprised at how much lower the temperature was than in the city I could still see sitting in the flat lands below.

There was a muttered exchange between Morelli and an officer who stepped forward to greet him before we were led, in silence, along a track that curved away behind some rocks before slowly descending the hillside. It would, I suspected, have led us all the way down to the farm that was the focus of our attention, but we stopped long before that, coming to a halt behind a tall, broad outcrop of boulders, amongst which sorry-looking shrubs and small trees attempted to grow.

With a signal to indicate that we must remain silent, we were directed into a narrowing gap between two of the boulders, which opened up on to a small flat piece of land fronted with an irregular row of smaller boulders. Morelli was handed a pair of binoculars and, stepping forward to position himself in an opening, he raised them to his eyes and looked down the gentle slope. Satisfied with what he had seen, he handed the binoculars to me and stepped to one side, so I could take his place.

It took me a moment to bring the binoculars into the

correct position, but once I did, I felt my heart leap and a smile crossed my face. There, some six hundred yards away, was a cluster of buildings, all of which looked in need of repair. A two-storey farmhouse, with a red-tiled roof, sat at the centre, around which were positioned a pair of tumbledown barns, a tiny building in a state of near total collapse and a row of small, narrow buildings in better condition, though what they might be for I could not guess.

The buildings themselves could be seen easily enough from our vantage point without the aid of the binoculars, but what would not have been so easy to see were the men who were moving about the place. Though they appeared to make much effort to stay out of the open spaces and to stick close to walls, they could still be clearly seen as they moved about. I counted four, each of whom bore the appearance of the Georgians I had met before.

I handed the binoculars to Bachini with a broad smile on my face. We had our quarry cornered, right enough, and now it was time to flush them out.

I turned to Morelli and, in a whisper, asked, "What now?"

"Now we close the net," he replied, with a steely glint in his eye.

A PLAN IS HATCHED

Our position was, Morelli assured me, a strong one. We had men stationed all around the perimeter of the farm, largely in spots similar to the one we occupied; rocky outcrops dotted with sparse undergrowth that provided enough cover from which to observe the farm with little likelihood of being seen. Further back, behind this inner ring, were other groups of police and soldiers, most of them guarding the few roads and tracks that passed through the area.

Our only real difficulty appeared to be the open ground closer to the farm buildings, across which we would have to pass, from whichever direction we approached. It seemed unlikely, in the extreme, that Von Luck and his Georgians would not have guards stationed for the precise purpose of spotting any approaching threat. But the Colonel's men had identified a potential solution to this difficulty.

Having consulted with the senior police officer, the Colonel turned to Bachini and me to explain their plan.

"As you can see, our greatest problem in reaching the farm is the open land between here and there. We would make easy targets for the Georgians long before we reached cover. But there is a shallow, narrow gully that runs up the hillside from the south-east and reaches almost to the first barn. Our plan is to send a dozen men up that gully to secure the barn. Once they have done that, we will send up more men to then secure the second barn. It is possible that from there we may be able to reach the farmhouse without being seen and take the Georgians by surprise. But it will make little difference, because once we have occupied those barns there will be no way out for Von Luck and his men. They can either surrender or face their fate."

"The Sultan's son?" I asked, with some concern. "Surely he will be at risk if we cannot achieve complete surprise?"

"I have a strong suspicion that our German friends are very keen not to harm the Sultan's son," answered Morelli, his nose twitching. "Even if they try to disown Von Luck, it will not be a good look for them if the Sultan's son is found dead at the hands of a German agent. I believe it has been their intention all along to get what they want from the Sultan and then let his son go free."

I pursed my lips, not altogether convinced by Morelli's view of the situation, but it was Bachini who spoke next.

"Even if the Colonel is wrong, Alexander, we cannot sit idly by. If the Sultan succumbs to the German's demands and allows the Kaiser's forces into Erteria, it will surely lead to war. We cannot pass up this opportunity to rescue his son."

There was a cold, calculating edge to her voice and a steeliness in her eyes that made me feel a little ashamed of my own hesitation.

"Yes, you are, of course, right," I replied.

"I would like to join the first group to make their way up that gully," declared Bachini, directing herself now at Morelli.

The Colonel thought on the request briefly before agreeing, then looked at me. I nodded. It was an opportunity I was not about to pass up and I felt the familiar tingle of nervous excitement. Action beckoned and I was ready for it, whatever it might bring.

THE NET CLOSES

Bachini and I found ourselves crowded together with a dozen armed police officers on a small patch of dusty ground that gave access to the gully we were about to negotiate. There was an unmistakable nervous tension about the group. Some checked and rechecked their weapons, one stood with his back against a boulder, his lips moving in silent prayer, while another re-tied the laces in his boots with a fastidiousness that made it clear the activity was an effort to distract his mind from what was about to happen.

I too felt that peculiar sensation that comes from a mixture of fear and excitement. Indeed, having realised I had begun to breath fast and shallow, it took some effort to slow and deepen my breathing.

Not long after Bachini and I joined the group, their officer gave a signal and we began to form up in readiness to enter the gully. I adjusted the collar of my shirt, straightened out my jacket then took a firm grip on the revolver I held in my right hand.

The gully, at the point we entered it, was wide enough for two men to walk side-by-side and sufficiently high to shelter us from observation by those in the farmhouse, so long as we took the trouble to stoop just a little. We had some trouble from the beginning with the broken nature of the ground, on which it was all too easy to stumble, especially in those parts where erosion had worn away heavily at the flanks of the gully. And in this confined space the rays of the

151

sun were held, not released, causing little patches of sweat to begin forming at my temples and in the pits of my arms.

We had gone barely more than fifty yards when the gully began to narrow markedly and to grow increasingly shallow. This required us to continue on in single file and to stoop ever lower as we did so, which made our progress hard work.

At one point I heard a stumble and then the sound of someone falling to the ground behind me and looked back to see an officer grimacing as he climbed back to his feet, rubbing at one knee. I paid even more attention to where I was putting my own feet as my heart beat increased rapidly as the tension grew.

We had travelled what I judged to be some hundred yards when our little column came to a halt. Our vanguard had just negotiated a sharp bend in the gully and were now out of sight of Bachini and me. We waited, hunched over in nervous silence, desperately aware of our exposed position. If we were seen and fired upon, it would be hard to escape back the way we had come. My lips had grown dry and I was forced to wipe the sweat from the palms of my hands on my trouser legs.

Several minutes passed before we recommenced our advance and, as we negotiated the sharp bend, we could see the cause of our delay. A large boulder that had been blocking our progress had needed to be moved aside, no small matter when this had to be achieved in near silence and without standing upright. I placed a hand on the boulder as we passed it, thankful I had not been one of those involved in the removal.

Our progress until this point had been up a noticeable incline, but now the ground began to flatten out until we were on no more than a gentle slope, little more than level ground. We were moving along on our hands and knees, for fear that to do otherwise would risk our being seen, and I was beginning to suffer from the rough, sharp edges of the stones over which we moved, cuts and abrasions stinging my exposed flesh.

Presently we stopped again and word travelled in whispers down the line that we were close to the first barn. I found my hand was shaking a little as I lifted it to wipe away the sweat that had begun to run down the side of my nose. I half expected that, at any moment, shouts of alarm would fill the air around us as a sentry saw our creeping advance. I swallowed in an effort to moisten my drying mouth.

My arms and legs were aching considerably by now and I longed to stretch out, to shake loose the knots that had been forming in my muscles. Even my neck had begun to ache and I tried my best to relieve that pain by rolling my head from side to side, but with little benefit.

But I had not long to wait until we were once more on the move, only this time things were different. The tension had grown considerably and I could see nervous faces up ahead of me as, one by one, those in front crept gingerly over the side of what remained of the gully and disappeared from view.

I was desperate to peer over the top to see where they were going, even though I knew they must be heading for the barn, and I realised my jaws had clamped so tightly together they were beginning to ache. I took a deep breath and tried to clear my mind.

Then I found myself at the head of the queue and it was my turn to slip silently over the top. The ground was no less littered with sharp-edged stones than it had been until this point and they nipped and tore at me as I struggled for a solid grip on the shallow edge of the gully. Looking up, I could see one of the officers duck through a narrow doorway into the barn. I could also see, to my relief, that we were not overlooked by the farmhouse.

I steadied myself, breathed in deeply, then pushed away, my shoes slipping briefly on the loose ground before giving me the grip I needed and I moved swiftly across the open space, hunched over, towards the barn some forty feet away.

Never has such a short distance seemed to take so long to cover. By the time I ducked through the doorway, it felt as if

I had been out there, in the open land between the gully and the barn, for an hour. My nerves were in tatters, my shirt wet with sweat and my hair glued to my skull it was so damp. It didn't matter that for a moment I could see little in the gloomy darkness of the barn; all I could think of doing was to press my back against a section of the stone wall and drop to the hard, cold ground, relieved to still be in one piece.

I had barely opened my eyes again when I felt someone drop down beside me and saw Bachini looking at me, a broad smile on her perspiring face.

"We made it," she said, sounding breathless and pleased.

THE ESCAPE

Our first objective had been achieved and there was a palpable sense of relief amongst our little group. Now it was time for the second group to move up the gully and secure the other barn. A signal was flashed back to our colleagues hidden amongst the scrub and boulders to the south-west, then we set about taking up what few positions we could that would allow us to provide covering fire, should it be needed. Since the gully did not reach as far as the second barn, it seemed unlikely we would be able to secure it as easily as we had the first.

I joined Bachini by the large closed wooden doors at the front of the barn. It was possible to get a view of the farmhouse by peering through one of the many gaps between the gnarled wooden frame of the doorway and the stone wall and we took advantage of this.

Outside the farmhouse, two burly fellows sat on an upturned wooden crate. They were smoking and apparently engaged in conversation. Fortunately for us what they were not doing was acting the part of effective sentries. Movement could also be made out inside the farmhouse, though it was not possible to pick out any details through the small windows. Bachini tapped me on the arm and indicated I should look towards our right. There I saw two more men advancing across the farm yard from out of scrub land that was, thereabouts, heavily populated with trees. As we watched them advance, to my horror I realised they were heading our way.

Bachini swung round and indicated to the senior police officer that men were approaching. We all froze, barely able to let ourselves breathe, and listened intently to the steady crunch of boots on stones. The noise seemed to grow to such proportions that it began to echo in my head, blotting out every other sound, save for the thumping of my heart.

The two men came to a halt right in front of the barn door, mere feet away from where I stood on the other side of the wall. I brought my revolver up in front of my chest, my index finger caressing the trigger guard, and tried to steady myself, ready for action. There was a violent shake of the doors that almost made me jump. Then it came again as the Georgians made sure it was securely locked. I licked my top lip as sweat began to form there and glanced at Bachini, whose wide eyes were staring intently at the handles on the doors.

One of the Georgians said something to the other, then came the now familiar sound of boots on gravel as the two men walked away, seemingly in the direction of the second barn. I puffed out my cheeks and lowered my gun to my side. Bachini looked across, smiled and fanned her face in an exaggerated manner with one hand.

After a minute or two, we were able to make out the two Georgians as they continued on their patrol, moving on from the second barn towards the broken land beyond. As they did so, word came to us that the next group of police had reached the top of the gully and were preparing to make a bid at reaching the other barn. The danger was that this entailed crossing a short section of open ground. If they were seen our element of surprise would be lost and they would be exposed to potential fire from the farmhouse. We readied ourselves as best we could, searching out better gaps in the stonework through which we could lay down covering fire.

For several minutes there was only silence, save for the occasional call from a bird passing overhead or the bleat of a sheep, several of which were scattered across some of the nearby fields. The two men sitting outside the farmhouse remained as unconcerned about anything other than their conversation as they had been when I first observed them.

The first gunshot, when it came, detonated in this near silence like exploding dynamite. I quite literally jumped with the shock as the sound echoed off the walls. Within seconds, as I struggled to regain my wits, there was an eruption of gun fire from what seemed to be every direction. I saw Bachini poke her revolver into a small gap alongside the frame of the barn door and begin firing in the direction of the farmhouse, no doubt aiming for the two men who had been sitting outside.

As voices began to call out all around and our own men opened up fire on whatever targets they could see, I pushed myself into action and peered out through another hole. Across the yard I could see one of the Georgians lying still on the ground, while his colleague was firing in our direction from the side of the farm building. Rifles were pointing out of the windows of the farmhouse, their muzzles flashing madly. Off to the right, I could just make out another force of soldiers and police advancing swiftly across a stretch of boulder-strewn ground. To our left I could see more figures squeezing in from that flank. The advance was swift and the net was closing quickly.

Bullets thudded into the ground and pinged off stonework seemingly in their hundreds as the gunfire continued unabated. The farmhouse was taking a particularly heavy amount of the fire, throwing up so many splinters of stone it began to form a haze in the air. I saw the Georgian firing from the side of the building slump to the ground, then another tumble from a small outbuilding away to the left. Surely surrender was now the only option for Von Luck and his men? There could be no way out for them.

Then, as if he had heard my thoughts and was keen to show me how wrong I was, four figures, one of whom was very clearly Von Luck, rushed out the side of the farmhouse and dashed towards a large outbuilding nearby. A burst of gunfire from our left sent one man to the ground, but the others reached the building and disappeared inside.

"Von Luck," I called across to Bachini.

She nodded and we immediately dashed for the narrow doorway through which we had entered the barn. It was a risky business going outside, but the reluctance I had about doing so soon evaporated. The doors on the building Von Luck had run into swung open violently and almost at once a motor vehicle roared out into the sunlight.

There was a brief burst of fire aimed at the vehicle, then it appeared to be left entirely alone. I was momentarily confused, until it occurred to me that our men had stopped firing in order to avoid injuring or even killing the Sultan's son.

"He's getting away," I shouted in frustration.

Surely, this time it was too much even for Von Luck to escape? Today of all days we would hold him in our clutches. But I couldn't ignore a sudden feeling of sickness that arose in my stomach as the possibility began to dawn on me that he might, indeed, be getting away.

A PAIR OF HUNTING HOUNDS

Bachini shook her head. "It's the Sultan's son," she yelled, as bullets continued to rain in on the farmhouse. "They dare not fire at the vehicle for risk of shooting him."

I cursed as I watched the motor vehicle bounce along the dusty track, heading away from us and towards the road. Surely the route would be blocked, but that soon mattered not for the vehicle suddenly lurched to the right and ran on across broken ground before disappearing behind an outcrop of boulders.

A bullet zipped off the stone of the barn close to my head as I stood looking on in disbelief at the cloud of dust left by Von Luck's escape. But Bachini had not yet given up and, shaking me by the arm, indicated I should follow her.

We ran back behind the barn and across the open land towards the spot where she knew Morelli would be waiting. But it wasn't him she was in search of. As we stumbled through the wall of boulders, Bachini pointed at a pair of motor vehicles parked in the shade of a stand of trees.

As we ran towards them, I called out helplessly, "But I can't drive one of those."

Bachini looked back and said simply, "I can."

Cranking the starter motor took a considerable effort, as I struggled to catch my breath, but soon enough I had joined Bachini in the vehicle and she was steering it down the track and back up on to the road. Once there, we were quickly flying along at a speed I thought certain would see us go

159

hurtling off the road and I clung to the body of the car in a limpet-like manner.

As we rounded a shallow bend, we caught sight of another police vehicle ahead of us, closing on a fork in the road. There was no sign of Von Luck and, after appearing to slow to assess his options, the police driver steered his vehicle down the left-hand turn. That made up Bachini's mind for her and, without so much as the merest pause, she threw our vehicle down the other fork and hurtled onwards, a great cloud of dust being thrown up behind us.

I tried to look back at the farm and the barns, but we had by now dropped down into a wide dell where we seemed to be cut off from the rest of the world, enclosed on all sides by higher ground. For a second, I did catch sight of two other vehicles that I thought were following along behind us, but then I realised they too must have taken the left-hand fork in the road, for they were climbing a gentle incline up the side of the hill.

Our vehicle bucked wildly as a wheel caught a large stone, unseen by Bachini, who clung desperately to the steering-wheel as she struggled to keep us on the earthen road. My head thumped against the metal bodywork as I was thrown to the side and it took all the effort I could muster not to then fall forward against the windscreen.

Then, as I sat back, I saw it, a flash of metalwork in the sunlight, some way up ahead.

"There, going up the slope," I called out, jabbing a finger in front of me. "It must be Von Luck's vehicle."

There was another glint of sunlight on metal before the vehicle disappeared over a gentle rise. Our own vehicle, which had slowed a little as Bachini regained control, surged forward with a roar and we were once again being bounced violently in all directions as we sped after our quarry.

"Let's make sure we get there in one piece," I bellowed over the sound of the engine, but Bachini merely glanced at me before returning all of her concentration to the road ahead.

We passed through a tight turn in the road where, as we were forced to slow, I found I could taste the dust left suspended in the air by Von Luck's vehicle. It was a welcome and most tangible sign that we were not that far behind and I looked ahead all the more eagerly.

As the road tumbled away steadily down the side of a shallow valley, it narrowed even more, twisting erratically between rocky outcrops and small stands of craggy trees. Eventually, even Bachini was forced to slow a little for fear of a collision, allowing me to slacken my grip somewhat on the door handle.

And it was then, as we rounded a generous curve that arced over a gentle incline, that we saw it, the vehicle we had been chasing. It had been abandoned at the side of the road, the doors left open, enveloped in a haze of gently drifting dust.

"There. It's them," I bellowed, needlessly, for Bachini had already seen it.

She brought our vehicle to a juddering halt alongside the other and we tumbled out at once.

"They must have hit a rock," I declared, with some excitement, pointing down at the front left wheel, which sat at a peculiar angle.

"They can't have gone far. They weren't a long way ahead," replied Bachini, as she began to scout the ground around us.

It was more scrub, not fit for farming, and heavily covered with rocks, boulders and isolated clumps of trees and shrubs that had begun to shed their autumn leaves. The temperature had climbed a degree or two as we had descended and crows called from the hillside up above us. There appeared to be no obvious route for Von Luck to have taken and we began to hurriedly survey the ground around us.

"Here," called out Bachini after a short while.

There were clear scuff marks in the dusty ground where men had passed through.

"They're still heading down," I pointed out. "Perhaps to some other refuge they have equipped in advance."

"Perhaps," she replied, as she checked her revolver. "In which case, let's make sure we catch up with them before they reach it."

We hurried off down the gentle incline, finding a steady trail of scuffed boot marks to follow, almost as if someone had made a point of signalling their passing that way. Perhaps the Sultan's son had kept his wits about him well enough to think of aiding our pursuit.

A flight of small birds passed rapidly overhead, as if keen to escape the heat of the sun, as we scrambled over a short, steep incline. As we strained our eyes in search of hurrying figures, we caught the glint of sunlight on moving water from the bottom of a shallow gorge.

"A river?" I asked, pointing ahead.

"Must be, though I don't know these hills," replied Bachini, pushing a stray lock of hair away from her face.

"There," I called out in great excitement. "A figure. And another. Passing through that clump of boulders a little to the left. They're heading for the river."

"I see them," replied Bachini. "Quickly. There could be boats down there."

We hurried on, stumbling on the uneven ground. I began to grow a little breathless and caught my knee on an old gnarled tree stump at one point, which sent a sharp stab of pain coursing through me. We lost sight again of our quarry as we descended, but pressed on as quickly as our feet would carry us, confident in our course.

I heard the river before I saw it again. Water tumbling through a section of fast-flowing rapids; more a pleasant gurgling than a thunderous roar. As we passed through a small wooded copse, the river began to open up before us. It curved round from our left, a modest affair, though plenty large enough to take a boat, the waters shallow and boulder-strewn on the inside, deeper and darker under an outer bank that stood a few feet higher.

A hand took me by the shoulder and shook me. Bachini brought her other hand up to her lips to signal silence, then pointed away to our right. There, partly hidden by a row of enormous bankside willows, the long dangling branches of which swayed gently in the breeze, sat a wooden boathouse that had clearly seen better days. It was large enough for a medium-size pleasure craft of the sort a family might take out for an afternoon's gentle cruise. Running alongside the riverbank on either side of it was a wooden jetty, its mellowed timbers baking gently in the sun.

A figure stood, unmoving, outside the boathouse, partially hidden in the shadow cast by the building. It appeared to be waiting for someone or something.

"To the left. By those reeds," whispered Bachini in my ear.

I struggled to make out what she had seen as I stared intently at a long, unbroken stretch of reeds that ran along the nearside bank by the jetty. Then a bird flew up from amongst them in alarm and I at once saw the figure of a man in a rowing boat. He was making his way towards the boathouse, pulling the oars with obvious care, so as not to draw unwanted attention.

"Got him," I replied, my voice low.

"That's not Von Luck," pointed out my colleague.

"No, it isn't. Perhaps that's him standing in the shadows," I suggested, thinking how appropriate that would be.

"I'll take the man in the boat," suggested Bachini. "You can have Von Luck."

I nodded, a thin smile appearing on my face. There were two of them and two of us, assuming the Sultan's son was incapacitated; tied up, perhaps. Those were odds I was more than happy to accept. Von Luck had a great deal to answer for and perhaps, just perhaps, this was the day when he would be brought to account. I felt the welcome weight of the revolver in my hand and tightened my grip on it just a little more.

"Happy shooting," said Bachini, as she stepped forward

towards the river, seeking out the generous cover of the bankside undergrowth.

She looked as keen as could be and I gave her quarry little chance of avoiding either capture or, should it come to it, certain death. She had debts of her own to settle.

A WELCOME CONFRONTATION

I watched Bachini go before I turned and moved away towards the boathouse, approaching from behind the patchy cover of the willows and other smaller trees that grew more densely by the river. If I could keep the element of surprise, I would, I hoped, be able to confront Von Luck without risk to the Sultan's son.

It was not easy going, the ground being uneven, pitted with hollows that I suspected had been worn out by flood waters. I frequently lost sight of the boathouse altogether and, even when it remained in view, I could not always see the stationary, shadowy figure standing in its shelter, which left me increasingly unnerved as I closed the gap.

Eventually, up ahead, I saw a narrow path leading down to the boathouse from somewhere up the hillside to my right. I assumed that somewhere above us there must be a road or some other track that provided access to the boathouse and river. But using the path would leave me exposed should the figure outside the boathouse turn around. Instead, I ducked down low and crept with care through the outer reaches of the undergrowth, aware that one careless step and the snapping of a branch might give me away in an instant.

At last I reached the cover afforded by the corner of the boathouse and, pressing myself up against its dry, rough flank, I peered with caution around the side at the figure now no more than twenty yards away. It was Von Luck, of that there was no doubt whatsoever. He was staring out across

165

the river, and his composed, unmoving posture was that of a man who felt calm and assured, not at all the panic-stricken individual most other men would have been in such dangerous circumstances.

The sight of the man, so close by, nauseated me. I recalled his arrogance at the ball, when we had been obliged to listen to his self-serving nonsense, and also the good men whose deaths he was responsible for. Anger and an overwhelming need to make the man pay for his deeds began to well up inside me and I struggled to keep control of myself.

How to fall upon him before he had an opportunity to react, that was my next challenge. The rest of the dirt path alongside the boathouse presented no problem, but then I had a section of wooden boarding to cross and that looked to be in rather poor condition. But it had to be done and moving quickly would serve me well. I brought my revolver up in front of my face and steeled myself for action. It was now or never and I intended to give everything I had.

I took a step forward, out into the open, and, almost at once, a shout went up from my left. It was a man's voice, deep and strong, and it cried out an alarm. I looked across, my eyes wide with fear. The suddenness with which the near silence had been broken was unnerving. I could just see the prow of a rowing boat poking out from where the reeds seemed to be at their thickest. Then the air was ripped asunder by an explosion of gunfire that seemed to erupt simultaneously from both the boat and the bank.

Turning back towards the river, I saw Von Luck, now alert and focused on the commotion to his left, take a step forward before raising his own revolver and taking a steady aim. Bachini! She would be hard pushed to avoid fire from two directions simultaneously.

I yelled a warning as loud as my lungs could manage then fired off two shots at Von Luck before he had begun to fire himself. Frustratingly, in my panic, I fired too hastily and my bullets flew out over the rushing waters of the river, missing my target by a comfortable margin.

Von Luck wheeled around, and, seeing me standing there, a sickening smirk appeared on his face as his finger squeezed the trigger on his revolver. I lurched forward as he did so and two bullets thudded into the bare ground alongside me.

Ignoring those, I rushed ahead, firing again at the arrogant German agent, who glanced away in the direction of the rowing boat before dashing from my view into the boathouse. I threw myself to the ground as I reached the corner of the building, with little more than the raised decking between me and the river. From my left came another burst of gunfire and now I could see more of the rowing boat, bobbing alarmingly in the water as a tall, well-built man with a thick, dark beard struggled to keep control as he fired into the undergrowth on the bank.

Peering intently in the direction he was firing, I saw a flash leap out from behind the cover of a willow tree as Bachini returned fire. Just then a bullet smashed into the timbers close to my head, sending splinters in all directions. I ducked in fright before swinging around the corner and firing off two shots of my own.

I got the briefest sighting of Von Luck, who was taking shelter behind a small outbuilding on the other side of the boathouse. My heart was racing as never before and my mouth had gone almost completely dry, but I reminded myself that I must keep a grip. Panic and fear were poor bedfellows in such a dangerous situation.

Another bullet exploded in the timbers at my feet and I immediately leaned around the corner and fired as well as I could towards the spot where I had seen Von Luck. I saw him duck for cover and, having noticed a thick, heavy upright beam a few feet away from me, I took the opportunity to dash towards it.

Breathing heavily, I opened the chamber of my revolver to see that I had but one bullet left and reached into a pocket for fresh rounds. As I did so, my attention was caught by the figure of a man who lay, tied and gagged, on the wooden floor at the rear of the boathouse. He stared back at me with something close to panic in his dark eyes and began to wriggle for all he was worth. The Sultan's son and still alive. That, at least, was a relief. I raised a hand and indicated he should lay still. For a moment I thought he was intent on ignoring me, but then he stopped moving and merely looked back at me.

Swinging back around the side of the beam, I loosed off two more shots in Von Luck's direction and was rewarded with the sound of a bullet thudding into the timber close by my head. I dropped back behind cover, realising that I was now shaking after such a close miss.

But the Sultan's son was very much within sight of Von Luck and there was no telling what such a cold-blooded creature might do in such circumstances. I had to push on. Force the German agent away from the boathouse.

I swung around the other side of the beam and fired again. But Von Luck had anticipated my manoeuvre and moved to the other end of the small shed-like structure he was hiding behind, leaving me firing at nothing but timber. Stepping out into the open, the better to take aim, he fired and a moment later I felt a searing pain at the top of my left arm as his bullet cut through my clothes and the edge of my flesh.

A shout of pain filled the space inside the boathouse and I fired a wild pair of shots in the general direction of Von Luck. But the German agent scented his moment of victory and went to fire again, with a composure that had so suddenly deserted me.

WHERE DEATH LINGERS

The air, however, remained silent. There was no explosion of gunfire, nor another shout of pain from me. Von Luck looked with disgust at his revolver before hurling it in to the river. He had run out of ammunition.

I felt at my arm and decided the wound was minor, the bullet having caught me no more than a winging shot. Swinging my revolver back towards the spot where Von Luck had stood, I saw him rushing off into the trees and fired again in his direction, but seemingly without luck, for he had soon disappeared from sight.

I cast another glance back at the Sultan's son to ensure he was still alright and then I was racing across the timber walkway, springy beneath my feet, and on into the trees beyond, raging at the thought Von Luck might escape me once more. Not this time. Even if it might mean my own demise, I was determined to put an end to his evil activities, once and for all.

Von Luck appeared to have raced off up a steady incline, through the cover of a stand of trees, and possibly into another of those rocky outcrops we had already passed in abundance in the hills. As I reached this semi-barren spot, I was breathing heavily and covered with a film of sweat.

I stopped at a narrow opening between two large flat-faced boulders. Leaning on one to steady myself, I took a deep breath then listened intently for some sign of my quarry. My only reward was the shrill call of birds and the gentle whisper of willow leaves as they shifted lazily in the breeze.

With no obvious sign as to which way Von Luck had gone, I skirted the edge of the rocky outcrop for a short distance on either side before becoming painfully aware that my enemy had turned the tables. It was he who now possessed the element of surprise. I returned to the spot between the two large boulders, wiped away a finger of sweat that had begun to run down the side of my face, then stepped forward, on to a narrow stony track that might have been worn away by passing animals.

In places the boulders I passed were sufficiently high that they blotted out most of the sights and sounds around me and I began to feel as I might be in an entirely different world, cut-off from everyone and everything else. It was an unnerving sensation that left me feeling uncomfortably alone and exposed. I tightened my grip on my revolver.

Presently I came to a small open space where a few tufts of straw-like grass sprouted from the thin soil and the sun shone more strongly on my face. To one side, I noticed the weathered skull of some small animal long since fallen prey to a hunter; an unnerving discovery that underlined my own situation.

Continuing across this open patch of ground, I passed through another cluster of rocks and boulders, the last of which reared up high above me. Stepping beyond this, I found myself facing another dense stand of trees, where the river moved swiftly by some hundred yards away to my left.

There was no sign of Von Luck, nor any indication he had been this way. I was perplexed and a little annoyed to think that my quarry had seemingly evaded me with such ease. I half-turned to retrace my steps when there was a movement above me, then a rush of air. As Von Luck dropped from the top of one of the tall boulders, he knocked me to the ground with a violent jolt, my revolver spinning from my grip.

A FINAL SHOWDOWN

I gasped for breath, confused and afraid, but instinctively rolled away to one side, before sweeping out a stiff, straight leg. I was rewarded for my efforts with a solid contact and a shout of pain as my boot made contact with Von Luck's shin. He stumbled backwards, his face scrunched up with pain. Struggling to regain my breath, I quickly scanned the ground around me, searching for my revolver, but found no sight of it. I leapt to my feet and brought my fists up in front of me, trying to remember the hand-to-hand combat training given by the Bureau's instructors during my first weeks as an agent.

Von Luck cursed before regaining his composure and taking up position opposite me. His brown eyes narrowed, in much the same way I imagine a fox's do when it spots a prospective meal, and a cold, unsettling smirk grew on his narrow, pale face. I became acutely aware that he was a little taller than me and had a somewhat longer reach. It might not be much of a difference, but it nonetheless gave him an advantage over me.

"So, it comes down to the two of us, eh, Templeman," he said, with a confidence I hoped to beat out of him. "How appropriate. It will allow me to repay you for your relentless interfering in my activities," he added, taking a half-step to his right.

I shifted a little to my left.

"You've got it all wrong, Von Luck. I've waited a long

171

time to make you pay for the fine men you've had killed and I'm not about to let the opportunity slip from my grasp now. Here is where you breathe your last breath."

He laughed, loud enough to cause birds in a nearby tree to take to the wing in startled alarm.

"Such arrogance from such a weak and insignificant man," he sneered. "It is your stiff and cold body that will be carried from this hillside, not mine."

With an alarming swiftness, Von Luck snatched up a solid length of tree branch from the ground by his feet and swept it in an arc as he lunged towards me. It was only by the narrowest of margins that I managed to jump aside and avoid the impact.

Another swift movement, unexpected from such a tall man, and Von Luck was attacking from my left. This time I felt the hard, gnarled branch catch the leg of my trousers as I struggled to step away.

I looked sharply about me, then snatched up a branch of my own. It was less impressive a weapon that Von Luck's, but it would have to do. We circled some more as my enemy feigned first one way then the other before rushing at me. Again I jumped aside, swinging my own weapon as I did so but finding nothing except empty air.

This time Von Luck did not step back before attacking again and instead lunged forward once more. I parried the first blow, but was too slow to deflect the second and the impact sent pain shooting up my left arm. Von Luck smiled and wiped the dust from his thick moustache as he set himself for another attack.

"You should let me put you out of your misery," he sneered. "A single blow to the head with a large stone should do it. So much better than making it a long, drawn out, painful affair."

I said nothing in return and tried to ensure my features did not give away my growing concern that I might be no match for him. He was, though, right to suggest he had the upper hand. I needed to try something new, or risk being beaten steadily into submission and, finally, death.

Von Luck lunged towards me once more, but this time I did not seek to evade him. Instead, I threw myself forward, swinging a fist towards his head. I caught him a fine blow on the side of the jaw, a welcome stab of pain inflaming my hand. He staggered back, temporarily shocked. I allowed him no time to regroup, launching myself at him again.

Knocking the branch from his grasp, I swung again for his chin; a blow he deflected. A knee thudded against my thigh and a fist buried itself in my stomach, as I landed a blow of my own close to his kidneys. We grappled, both hissing and cursing, as we struggled to gain the upper hand. All the while I kept him as close to me as I could manage, stripping away the advantage of his longer reach.

A hardened toe cap bit into my shin and, suddenly breathless, I slumped a little towards the ground on the one leg, in danger of falling. But as I did so, I swept a fist upwards, inside of Von Luck's guard, landing it violently on his chin. He wobbled, staggered back then dropped to the ground, supporting himself with an outstretched hand.

I reached down for the branch my opponent had let go and felt its solid weight in my hand. There was a time when I wouldn't have had the nerve to finish a man off in such a ruthless manner, but experience had shown me there are evils in this world that no sensible man can allow to continue. To do so leads only to more suffering and anguish. I took a deep breath and stepped forward.

As I did so Von Luck, shaking the fog from his head, reached out to the ground behind him, searching for something, anything, with which to defend himself. The sickening smile that appeared on his face was so alarming it caused me to stop.

His right hand swept round and in its grip was my revolver. I swallowed, my glance shifting from the weapon to Von Luck's face and back again as he got gingerly to his feet. He rubbed at his chin where my fist had made contact.

"Quite an impressive upper-cut you have there,

Templeman. Such a shame the world will see no more of it, but I've had enough of this ridiculous grappling. The Kaiser has put his trust in me and I am not going to let him down. Goodbye, Templeman."

He raised the revolver as he took aim at my head and I closed my eyes as I began to say a silent apology to my wife, Caroline, asking for her forgiveness.

The near silence of the woodland was ripped apart by the explosion of a gun being fired, not once but twice. But I felt no violent impact, nor surge of fatal pain as life was taken from me. I opened my eyes and was astonished to see Von Luck staggering backwards, wide eyes staring at the two stains of red that grew on the front of his dirty, damp shirt.

He looked up, directly at me, then, with a feeble effort, began to raise his gun in my direction. Once more, the air echoed to the explosion of gunfire. It was, I now realised, coming from behind me and this time Von Luck let go his grip on my revolver before slumping to the ground in a silent, twisted heap.

"Are you alright?" asked Bachini, her voice soft and calm.

I nodded in silent confirmation before dropping to my knees, close to tears as relief overwhelmed me. I had come so desperately close to death. Closing my eyes, I began to say a silent prayer, promising to shower Caroline with all the love I possessed and to take her somewhere far, far away from the dangers of the world. I reached up and held the hand that Bachini placed on my shoulder, whispering my thanks to her.

THE HORN OF AFRICA

We were standing on a broad marble terrace, dotted here and there with fine specimen lemon trees, the scent of which could just be picked out in the air, while a blazing sun shone down from out of a deep blue sky and a welcome, cooling breeze blew in from off of the sea, some five miles to the east. Behind us, vast in size and its plastered facade shimmering in the heat, was the Sultan of Zanzire's primary palace on the edge of his capital, Addis Mara.

I had never before visited the Horn of Africa and had found the previous two days a most eye-opening and extraordinary affair as Bachini and I travelled from one sight and experience to another, accompanied by one of the Sultan's personal assistants, acting as a most able guide. We had even plucked up the courage to risk a ride on one of those infamously ill-tempered beasts, the camel, though I was more than ready to dismount when the time came.

After the affair with Von Luck and his Georgians had been concluded and the relieved Sultan was re-united with his son, the conference had recommenced. It did not take long to conclude. Despite the German government's insistence that Von Luck had been acting on his own initiative and they had no forewarning of what he had planned, the Sultan's mind had already been made up. He brusquely dismissed the offer of a new loan from the Germans and, instead, accepted the one put forward by the Italians.

The German delegation left on the Monday morning, in a dark mood, muttering about bad faith and consequences. Of course, their failure at the conference was entirely their own fault, brought about by their arrogance and bullying behaviour. It had been Sir George Spence's opinion that, had they acted in good faith and carefully mined the warm relationship they had already established with the Sultan, they would more than likely have emerged from the conference with some form of triumph.

In matter of fact, in an effort to provide the German delegation with something positive to take back to their Kaiser, the other Great Powers present had gifted them with a few crumbs of comfort. Their merchant navy was to be allowed to make some use of Erteria's sole deep-water port and a commission was to be set up to look at how else their trade interests might be assisted to expand within the Sultan's realm. It was, in reality, little more than they already enjoyed but it did, at least, offer to formalise such arrangements.

With a new agreement reached, the Sultan, his eye on an opportunity to impress his own people, had insisted the loan and the attached diplomatic arrangements be signed in a grand ceremony at his palace. Naturally, a large contingent of press people had been shipped in from his own lands, those of the Great Powers and many others beside to witness the occasion.

Delighted at our rescuing of his son, the Sultan had invited Bachini and I to join him as his personal guests at this splendid affair, an opportunity we were both delighted to accept. Vivian Eastwood had questioned whether or not it was appropriate for an agent from the Bureau to attend such a high profile ceremony, but Sir Joshua had immediately overruled him, entirely content that I enjoy such a reward. He also thought it no bad thing that I garnered a little experience of life on the Horn and began to build contacts there that might prove useful in the future.

*

Colonel Morelli, looking somewhat overly warm in his full dress uniform, joined Bachini and me, emerging from a doorway that led out on to the terrace from one of the dozens of rooms in the palace. He had arrived the previous afternoon with the bulk of the Italian delegation and we had, thus far, spent little time in his company.

"This heat is too much," he said, fiddling at the collar of his shirt. "Even for someone born and raised in Sicily, the intensity of the sun here is overwhelming."

"Imagine what it is like for an Englishman such as myself," I replied, smiling broadly.

Indeed, Bachini and I had made a point of standing in the shade of one of the larger lemon trees, which afforded us a little protection from the sun.

"The Sultan can't stop saying how grateful he is to the two of you for rescuing his son," continued the Colonel. "I mentioned, of course, that over two thousand members of the Italian police and army were also involved in the rescue, but he prefers to believe that it was all down to the personal efforts of the two of you. And I, for one, am not about to risk his displeasure by attempting to persuade him otherwise."

"I may have played my part," I offered, feeling a little awkward. "But if not for Bachini then I would not be here myself and Von Luck might still be at large. Her intervention could not have come a moment later."

"I had been standing and watching the whole time," Bachini quipped. Then, when I looked aghast, she added, with a smile, "I'm only teasing, Alex. I arrived in that clearing only moments before Von Luck picked up your revolver."

"Well, whatever the truth of the matter," said Morelli, "the Sultan credits the two of you with the rescue. I heard from one of his men that he is thinking of awarding you both a medal."

Morelli's face showed his displeasure at this idea and I could imagine Sir Joshua taking a similar view. The two men would no doubt be of the view that all Bachini and I had done was our jobs and there was something to be said for that.

"My counterpart in Germany is still insisting that Von Luck acted entirely on his own initiative," said Morelli, pushing deeper into the shade of the lemon tree. I could see little patches of sweat glistening at his temples. "I told him he was a fool if he really thought I was going to believe that, but I suppose that will be the official story our government will put about, since it will be all but impossible to show proof of the truth."

"What about the Georgians?" I asked. "And especially Gregor Lomidze. Did you establish whether or not he was in Rome, leading his men?"

"His men we have locked up and they are bad-tempered and unhelpful. Perhaps they will change their minds when they realise that the alternative to co-operating is to risk swinging from the end of a rope after they have been found guilty of murder by an Italian jury. As for your friend, Gregor Lomidze, we have not been able to discover if he was in Rome. Indeed, there is currently nothing to be seen of the man anywhere."

"Gone into hiding, I imagine," suggested Bachini.

"No doubt he will show up somewhere else soon enough," replied Morelli.

"Yes, I strongly suspect you are right about that, Colonel. He is not the sort of man to remain in hiding for long. His temperament doesn't allow for it."

The sound of voices began to spill out of the palace from behind us and we turned to see what was going on. Erected on a large expanse of open ground in part of the palace gardens was an enormous tent in the Arab style. Positioned beneath it was a large table, along the back of which were a dozen chairs, the central one a much grander affair than the others. Indeed, it was almost throne-like.

Lined up in a row in front of the tent, exposed to the full force of the afternoon sun, was a row of photographers and press men, looking somewhat harassed in the heat. They had burst into a bout of energetic action, the cameramen adjusting and re-adjusting their cameras, convinced a minor shift here or there might make all the difference between a successful shot and a poor one.

The cause of this expenditure of energy was the sight of a body of men emerging from the palace. The Europeans were resplendent in their uniforms and suits, while the Sultan's sizeable entourage wore native attire. The more senior of them began to take their seats at the signing table.

There was, for a moment, one figure missing, but then the Sultan stepped out and all around him fell into a deferential silence as they waited for him to take his seat. Unlike his fellow countrymen, the Sultan was not wearing native dress. I knew already that he had attended a good public school in England and was most keen on leading his country forward into the new world; a modern world, though one that must exist alongside the tradition and religion of his peoples.

He wore a fine-looking European suit and black shoes that might have made him appear no different to those Europeans standing nearby. However, over the suit he wore a myriad of gold adornments, including a long necklace on which hung a large brooch that had been presented to him personally by Queen Victoria. On his head he wore the one item of native dress that he insisted on, a tightly-wrapped turban that rose to a modest peak at the front. However, most noticeable of all was the ring he wore on the little finger of his left hand; it held a large diamond that has been passed down from sultan to sultan since the early nineteenth century.

He was a tall man with something of a paunch, his face sporting a thick grey beard and slender moustache. Perhaps unsurprisingly, he bore the posture of a man of power and importance, a natural confidence that comes with such a position in life.

Only after he had taken his seat at the table did the rest of the party do likewise, the Italian Foreign Minister taking the seat to the Sultan's left. After a moment's conversation, the Sultan picked up a sizeable and rather extravagant quill, held it steadily over the large document on the table in front of him and looked out with assurance at the men of the press. Camera bulbs fired and pencils swept across paper as he sat still, providing them with all the time they needed to capture the moment.

*

As the cameramen folded away their ungainly equipment and the reporters slipped their notepads back into their pockets, Morelli gave a sigh and reluctantly announced he must now join the formal gathering, which would shortly be heading back inside. We had heard the meal that was shortly to follow was to be a rather spectacular affair, replete with local delicacies, about which I was most curious.

Morelli, it seemed, would have preferred to give up his place at the dining table and return at once to the familiar embrace of his beloved Italy. But he had to endure one more day on the Horn before he could do that.

Bachini and I were in no particular hurry to join the throng Morelli made for and, instead, we turned our gaze towards the sea, still glistening in the sunlight. Early in the morning, when the sun had yet to fully climb over the horizon, I had watched as a small flotilla of fishing boats had made their way back into the tiny harbour. Now, however, there was no sign of human activity on the water; the heat was too oppressive, even for the natives.

"It's such a lovely country. I could very happily spend a good deal of time here, exploring as much of the place as possible," said Bachini, shifting the rim of her hat a little. "Except, of course, I would soon miss London's tea shops and Rome's cafes."

"Perhaps the Sultan would help you find some suitable

premises so you could open your own tea shop here," I replied, mischievously.

Bachini smiled. "Running my own tea shop is something I have in mind for when I have retired from the service, raised a family and am in need of something else to do," came her amused response.

"Really? Then I shall look forward to being one of your first customers," I replied, smiling. "But please make sure you open it somewhere in Europe. Beautiful though it is here, it is also unbearably hot."

We stood in silence for a while, enjoying a little strengthening of the sea breeze. It was Bachini who eventually broke the silence.

"I wonder what the future holds for the Sultanate and how things might look here in ten or twenty years' time? From what we've seen of him, the Sultan's son doesn't seem to be half as impressive as his father and there are so many dangers to be faced."

"Indeed. The son doesn't seem to have the same level of intelligence, guile and aptitude for hard work as his father. That's always one of the disadvantages of not having a parliamentary democracy; you're entirely dependent upon the quality of the individual who inherits the throne next," I suggested. "There again, perhaps the closer relationship with your countrymen that should follow the new agreement that's been signed today will help protect them from some of the worst currents that might otherwise sweep them away."

"I fear it will take more than that to keep the Sultanate in one piece for much longer, especially in the current climate" replied Bachini. "I suspect the Sultan's efforts to modernise his territories will be a case of too little too late."

A gull drifted across the sky, high above the palace, riding the thermals with a practised skill as it let out a series of sharp, piercing cries. We both looked up and watched it drift out of sight.

"Have you heard the news from the Balkans?" asked Bachini. "The Serbs appear to be treating the people in their newly-conquered territories to the south terribly badly."

"Yes, I have heard a little about that. It seems as if the suffering of the people who live in that part of the world will never end. Though I fear also the Serbs will now look to press their claims to Bosnia-Herzegovina, which the Austrians are certain to resist, even at the risk of war."

"It feels sometimes," replied Bachini. "As if we are living at a time when despots and mad men are seeking to run the world to strife and ruin, all so they can snatch a few more fields and towns from their neighbours. I can only hope that more sane people will eventually prevail."

I was not altogether sure that I could be even as optimistic as that. My mind cast back to more ancient times, to the days of the Egyptians and to Rome's magnificent empire, then on to our own glory. Nothing lasts forever and change was and is the one and only constant in the world. One day another empire will rise to domination, for good or for bad, and all that we can hope is that, in the process, civilisation is able to stand up to the violent storms that will always sweep over it. The alternative is too dire to contemplate.

A voice called across the terrace from the palace, summoning us to join the celebratory feast. Without another word, Bachini and I turned and made our way across the sparkling marble terrace, towards the sound of conversation and laughter. For now at least, all was well with the world.

The End